almost identical

Twice as Nice

almost identical

Twice as Nice

by Lin Oliver

Grosset & Dunlap
An Imprint of Penguin Group (USA) LLC

GROSSET & DUNLAP
Published by the Penguin Group
Penguin Group (USA) LLC, 375 Hudson Street, New York, New York 10014, USA

USA | Canada | UK | Ireland | Australia | New Zealand | India | South Africa | China

penguin.com
A Penguin Random House Company

Cover illustration by Mallory Grigg

Text copyright © 2014 by Lin Oliver. All rights reserved. Published by Grosset and Dunlap, a division of Penguin Young Readers Group, 345 Hudson Street, New York, New York 10014. GROSSET & DUNLAP is a trademark of Penguin Group (USA) LLC. Printed in the USA.

Library of Congress Cataloging-in-Publication Data is available.

ISBN 978-0-448-46447-3 (pbk)   10 9 8 7 6 5 4 3 2 1
ISBN 978-0-448-46448-0 (hc)   10 9 8 7 6 5 4 3 2 1

For my Third Act sisters who inspire and delight—LO

A Weird Encounter

Chapter 1

"Hey, Charlie, you've got to come outside right now and check this out," my older brother, Ryan, yelled, pounding on my bedroom door. "It's the weirdest thing I've even seen!"

I was sitting cross-legged on my bed, deeply engrossed in applying a second coat of fluorescent lime-green polish to my nails.

"What could be weirder than you?" I hollered back, suspecting that this was just another one of Ryan's practical jokes.

I held out my hand to examine the effect. Perfect. The green was so bright that I practically needed sunglasses to look at it. Usually, I prefer a more neutral shade, like light pink or pale silver. When I'm feeling bad, though, I go for bolder colors. My twin sister,

Sammie, says she can tell my mood from my nails—the brighter the color, the worse my mood. So my choice of the smoking-hot fluorescent lime-green polish should tell you something about how miserable a mood I was in.

"Okay, fine," Ryan said. "Stay in there. I guess you don't want to see how totally insane Lauren is acting."

I jumped off my bed, practically tripped over my own feet, and flung open the door.

"Did you say Lauren?" I asked, waving both my hands urgently in the air so the polish would dry faster.

"Yeah. She's out on the tennis court, acting like a chicken. Clucking and everything."

"Wait. You don't mean Lauren Wadsworth, do you?"

Lauren was definitely not the kind of person who would go around clucking like a chicken for no reason.

"Yeah. Lauren Wadsworth. As in your ex–best friend. Remember her?"

I didn't appreciate his sarcasm. Of course I remembered her. It had been three weeks since Lauren and I had stopped talking, but I thought about her every day and wished we were still friends. My grandma GoGo says it's really hard to lose a best friend. No matter what your problems were or what you fought about or how much you believe you were right and she was wrong. Because the sad fact is that one day you have a best friend and the next day you don't. Trust me, that can put a person in a really miserable mood, one that even the brightest green nail polish can't fix.

"Are you positive it's Lauren?" I asked Ryan.

"I guess there's always the possibility that it's a mutant clone of her."

Very funny. Score another sarcastic comment for Ryan.

He had to be wrong. I knew it couldn't be Lauren. Sammie, and her Truth Tellers friends Alicia and Sara, might think it was hilarious to walk around clucking like a chicken or growling like a tiger. But they're drama kids—and they're always coming up with weird stuff to do. Lauren is a whole other kind of person. She's cool and popular and beautiful. The total opposite of weird. She wouldn't go clucking around unless she had lost her mind or something.

"I don't believe you."

"Come see for yourself, Charles. She's right in the middle of the tennis court."

"Okay," I said, "but I'm warning you, Ry. If this is one of your lame practical jokes, I'm never speaking to you again."

"Is that a threat or a promise?" he answered, cracking himself up.

I slipped into my flip-flops, gave one last wave of my hands, and ran out of my room. Following Ryan, I zoomed out of the house onto the deck and headed to the tennis courts, which are between the house and the beach. By the way, don't get the idea that we're rich enough to live on the beach with our own private tennis court or anything. We live in the caretaker's cottage at the Sporty Forty Beach Club in Santa Monica, California, where my dad is the tennis teacher while my Mom is away at cooking school. The forty families who belong to the club, like the Wadsworths, now they're rich. We, on the other hand, are totally not.

As I raced past the kitchen, I caught sight of GoGo and some girl out of the corner of my eye.

"What's the rush?" GoGo called out to me through the open window. "Come meet Bethany."

"I will later, GoGo," I answered without losing a step.

When I neared the tennis courts, I suddenly realized that I needed a plan. I couldn't just barge out there and ask Lauren what was up with the chicken thing. She probably wouldn't answer me. After all, we still weren't speaking.

What had happened between us was no little fight—it was major. I had told the police that Sean and Jared, two of her best friends, had started a bonfire at the beach that almost burned the neighbor's house down. They got in big-time trouble. I felt I had to tell the truth, but Lauren didn't think so. She said that the kids in the SF2s—her group, which until a couple weeks ago used to be my group, too—were loyal to each other, no matter what. They didn't rat each other out. Since then, she hasn't spoken to me, and neither have most of the other SF2s, except for Lily March and, thankfully, Spencer Ballard, the cutest boy in the entire seventh grade.

I decided to crouch down behind a bush. Craning my neck, I peeked through the chain-link fence that surrounds the two tennis courts. I couldn't see the whole court, just Lauren standing by the net, dressed in her usual great-fitting jeans and a yellow tank top that matched the gold highlights in her hair. She looked totally normal.

"See? What'd I tell you?" Ryan whispered as he crouched down next to me. "She's crazy, isn't she?"

"She's not doing anything even remotely crazy," I whispered back. "You're the crazy one."

But before he could say anything, Lauren put her hands on her hips, bent her arms at the elbow and started moving them back and forth like a chicken flapping its wings. Then she took off strutting around the court, poking her head in and out, the way a chicken does when it walks.

"Hey, Lauren, I don't hear you clucking," a girl's voice called from the open kitchen window.

"Bethany, do I have to?" Lauren whined. "It's so embarrassing."

"We all did it!" the girl named Bethany shouted back. "You can, too."

"Cluck, cluck, cluck," Lauren said, sounding like a really angry chicken.

Bethany howled with laughter. "Keep going, Lauren. I'll let you stop when I'm finished talking to the cook here."

What cook? I thought. Then I realized that Bethany was the girl in the kitchen who was talking to GoGo. It happens that GoGo is a great cook—her guacamole is to die for—but she does not *work* at the club as a cook. She helps plan the parties and events, which is an entirely other thing.

"Who does she think she is, calling GoGo the cook?" I whispered to Ryan.

"Obviously one of the rich kids who belong here," he said. "They think everyone works for them."

"That girl isn't a member. I've never seen her here before."

"Me neither," he said, trying to peer into the kitchen. "But my eyes are happy they're seeing her now."

He made one of those boy hoots, the sound guys make when they see someone way too pretty for them to even talk to. The sound attracted Lauren's attention, and she strutted over to the fence where we were crouched.

"Who's there?" she asked, pointing her face in our direction.

I crouched lower but Ryan stood up.

"Ryan!" I heard Lauren giggle. She has a huge crush on my brother and likes to think that he has a huge crush back. "How long have you been here?"

"Long enough to see you do this," Ryan said. Then he immediately went into his imitation of Lauren imitating a chicken.

"Oh no!" she said. "Please forget you ever saw that. It's definitely not my best look."

"I didn't mind it," Ryan answered. "I like chickens. I usually like them fried with mashed potatoes on the side, but apparently, that's not your style."

"I can explain this whole thing," Lauren said.

"I hear you talking, Lauren," Bethany interrupted from the kitchen. "That's against the rules. Only clucking until I say you can stop."

Lauren dropped her voice to a low whisper. "I'm trying out for a club," she explained, just loud enough so Ryan could hear. Of course, I could hear, too, but she couldn't see me.

"And this club," Ryan said. "Is it just for people who impersonate chickens, or do you guys allow other poultry in, too? I do a mean duck quack."

"No, silly," Lauren said in the flirtiest tone of voice you've ever heard. "The club is called The Waves. My cousin Bethany is president."

"The Waves? Oh yeah. That spirit club at the high school—the one with all the hot girls who come to the football games and cheer?"

"Yup, that's it. And Bethany might let me start a Junior Waves at Beachside. But first I have to be initiated, which includes acting like a chicken until she says I can stop."

"Ahh . . . initiation by clucking," Ryan said. "That's girl logic for you."

Lauren laughed. She has this high giggle that

makes you want to laugh right along with her. I remember the first night I slept over at her house and we tried on her mom's gold jewelry and took pictures of ourselves trying to look very sophisticated. I laughed so much my stomach hurt.

I shifted my position behind the bush, suddenly aware that my leg was falling asleep. As I moved my foot, I thought I felt something crawling on it. Looking down, I saw the biggest spider you have ever seen walking up my ankle. It wasn't a sweet little spider like Charlotte, but a huge brownish thing with a shiny body and long purple-tinted legs. And those legs were crawling past my ankle and up to my knee.

Have I mentioned that I hate spiders? Well, I do.

I couldn't control myself. I jumped up and started screaming like I was being attacked by a zombie. I pulled off my sweatshirt and wildly swatted at my leg with the sleeve. I could hear myself yelling in this really panicky way, but I couldn't stop myself until I finally knocked the spider off my leg and it dropped to the ground. It was only then that I realized Lauren was staring at me with a nasty look on her face.

"Hi, Lauren," I muttered.

"Why were you spying on me?" she accused.

"I wasn't spying."

"Oh really? Then what do you call it? And just so you know, my conversation with Ryan doesn't concern you, so I'd appreciate it if you'd just leave."

"Whoa there," Ryan said. "Charlie lives here.

Where's she supposed to go?"

"Anywhere, as long as it's away from me," Lauren told him.

Just then, I heard the kitchen screen door slam, and turned around to see a girl who I assumed was Bethany bouncing over to the tennis courts. Okay, she wasn't actually bouncing, but her hair sure was. She had the thickest, shiniest, bounciest hair I'd ever seen—like Lauren's, only black instead of blonde. Those Wadsworths must have invented the gene for great hair. GoGo followed behind her, leaning on her fancy cane, the one with the carved pink flamingoes for a handle. GoGo's been staying with us ever since she broke her leg in a car accident, and even though she's up and around now, she still needs a little help walking.

"Well, how nice to see you girls talking," she said, sounding all cheery.

"The conversation is officially over," Lauren snapped.

GoGo could feel the hostility in the air. You'd have to be some kind of alien not to. Lauren was looking at me like she wished I would drop through a hole in the ground and disappear. Good ole GoGo, though, she tried to come up with some chatty things to say. She actually believes that if you're nice to people, they'll be nice back to you.

"Well, Bethany and I certainly got a lot accomplished," she said. "We planned the whole theme and menu for her sweet sixteen party. Wait until you girls hear about it."

"I'm totally stoked," Bethany said.

"The theme is very clever," GoGo said. "It's going to be 'Hats Off to Bethany.'"

"Let me guess," Ryan said. "Are all the guests going to wear hats?"

"How'd you know?" Bethany asked.

"Ryan is really smart," Lauren said.

Let me just point out here, unlike Sammie and I, who get good grades, Ryan is a straight-C student. The only person who would say he is "really smart" is someone who has a total crush on him.

"The hats are only the beginning," Bethany gushed on. "We're going to give everyone a crazy-fun hat and then at exactly the time I was born, 10:51 p.m., everyone's going to take off her hat and throw it in the air. Lily March is helping me design them. She's really talented, even though she's just a middle-schooler."

"Lily is an amazing clothes designer," I piped up. "She has her own special look."

"So," Bethany said, looking me up and down, as if it finally occurred to her that she wasn't the only person there. "Who are you, exactly?"

"Bethany, meet my granddaughter Charlie," GoGo said. "I assumed you two girls knew each other."

"Oh, so you're one of the twins," Bethany said to me. "Are you the one who used to be Lauren's friend? Or is that your sister?"

"No, that would be me," I said.

Bethany rolled her eyes, looked at her watch and sighed. "They're late," she announced.

"Who? Your royal coach and driver?" Ryan joked.

Lauren giggled, but Bethany clearly was not amused. "No. My parents. They have to go over my party details with the staff."

"I guess that means me," GoGo said, with a little edge in her voice. "If you kids will excuse me, the staff has to review the benefits of sliders versus mini pizzas." Then looking at me, she added, "I'm sure you girls have a lot to discuss as well."

I knew GoGo didn't have to leave that minute, but I figured she thought that if we kids were left alone, we would start a fun conversation and before you know it, Lauren and I would be talking again. GoGo always says that anger doesn't last, but friendship does.

Well, she was wrong this time.

"Come on, Bethany," Lauren said, the minute GoGo was gone. "We have better things to do than hang out with *her*. Ryan, you can come with us."

"Not so fast, Lauren," Bethany said. "I don't believe I've given you permission to stop clucking and strutting."

"You said I could stop when you got here," Lauren said.

"I said you could stop when I told you could stop. And I haven't yet."

"Bethany, please," Lauren begged.

"No whimpering, little cousin," Bethany said. "If you want to be in The Waves, you have to do what the president says. You'll understand that when you're president of the Junior Waves. You'll want everyone to follow what you say, too."

Lauren looked really annoyed but didn't say anything. Ryan, Mr. Sensitive, filled the silence with a series of duck quacks. Lauren forced a little laugh, but Bethany was not amused. I couldn't blame her for that. Giving Ryan a *grow up, you dork* look, Bethany gathered her hair into a ponytail. I noticed that she was wearing this soft gray-lavender nail polish, and suddenly, I felt like a total idiot for having neon-green nails. It's like my nails were screaming, *"Charlie Diamond is a total dork, too!"*

"Okay," Bethany said to Lauren. "I'm going to give you a break this time. No more chicken, but only if you go into the kitchen and get me a cold bottle of peach iced tea and bring it to our table."

"There are only two tables on the whole deck," Ryan pointed out. "You guys get one all to yourselves?"

"Do you have a problem with that?" Bethany answered, without even looking at him.

"No," Ryan said. "For all I care, you can sit wherever you want. I'm going for a run on the beach anyway."

"I'll take you as far as the kitchen," Lauren said, hooking her arm in his. The two of them trotted off together, leaving me there staring at Bethany.

Now that Lauren was gone, I thought maybe she'd be nicer to me.

"So I'll bet it's really cool to be in The Waves," I began in my nicest tone of voice.

"Of course it is," she snapped. Then she turned and headed toward "her" table.

I followed. I shouldn't have, I know. I should have just gone back to my room. I shouldn't have cared whether she liked me or not, but I think I was secretly hoping that she would find me so sweet and fun that she would tell Lauren how wrong she was to end our friendship.

"Charlie is such a great girl," I imagined her saying. *"Anyone would want to be her friend."*

I caught up to her, my brain racing to try to think of something cool to say.

"I hear you guys have your own Wave T-shirts and do special cheers at all the football games," I said, forcing a grin. "That must be a total blast."

"It is," she answered. "Too bad you'll never know."

That was it. End of conversation. We had reached her table, and Bethany sat down on one of the red-and-white striped beach chairs, reached into her purse and pulled out her sunglasses. She put them on, then turned her face up to the sky, basking in the warm rays of the early afternoon sun. I just stood there watching her ignore me, feeling even more miserable than I had before.

Trust me, friends. Being left out hurts.

Excluded

....

Chapter 2

"Well, this is an interesting twosome," Lauren said, skipping out of the kitchen and handing Bethany her iced tea.

Bethany pushed her sunglasses up to the top of her head, and turned to stare at me.

"Are you still here?" she asked. "Don't you have something better to do than to stand there looking all pathetic?"

I wanted my feet to move, to take me back to my room, away from the embarrassment of the moment. But it was like I was glued to the spot.

"Honestly, Lauren," Bethany went on, as she unscrewed the bottle top and took a delicate swig of the frosty drink. "I can't imagine how on earth you two were friends."

"Oh, that was forever ago," Lauren answered.

"Three weeks," I said quietly. "It was three weeks ago yesterday."

Lauren sat down on the chair next to Bethany and threw her long tan legs up on the table.

"Whatever," she said. "You'll have to excuse me if I'm not a human calendar like you."

She and Bethany both laughed, and I felt about the size of an ant. Any normal person would have just left, but not me. I started talking a mile a minute, which I do when I get nervous. I either freeze up completely and can't think of a thing to say, or I talk nonstop. There's nothing in between.

"Honestly, Lauren, you can't even imagine how bad I feel about everything that happened," I rambled. "I didn't like telling on Sean and Jared. I know you guys think I wanted to get them in trouble, but that's just not true. They're my friends, too."

"Were," she said tartly.

"But if I hadn't told the truth," I jabbered on, "Alicia's cousin Oscar would have been blamed for what Sean and Jared did. And then he would have been sent back to El Salvador and never would have gotten the operation he needed on his leg. I couldn't live with myself if that had happened."

"Oh, really?" Lauren said, whirling around to face me. "Well now look at what you've done to Sean and Jared."

She pointed toward the beach where the far end

of the deck meets the sand. Sean and Jared were both on their hands and knees, applying varnish to the redwood planks. They were wearing their baseball caps and Oakleys, so you couldn't see much of their faces, but you didn't have to. You could tell from their body language that they were not happy, to say the least.

"Thanks to you, they have to spend every weekend of the next two months doing all sorts of grungy chores around here," she said. "Weeding the garden and folding the towels and refinishing the deck. It's so embarrassing."

"They're helping Candido and Esperanza," I told her. "I don't see what's so embarrassing about that."

Candido is the groundskeeper at the club, and his wife, Esperanza, cleans and helps in the kitchen. Their daughter Alicia goes to Beachside with us and has become one of Sammie's best friends.

Lauren put her hands on her hips and spoke to me in the tone of voice you would use to explain kickball rules to a first-grader.

"Candido works here," she declared. "He is *not* a member. He will *never* be a member. Sean and Jared, on the other hand, *are* members. Their parents and grandparents have been in the Sporty Forty since before they were born. They shouldn't be doing the kind of work Candido does. It's just not right."

"And I suppose it's right to set a house on fire?" an angry voice said from behind me. "Because that's what your so-called friends did."

I whipped around to see Alicia standing there. She had obviously overheard what Lauren said, and I couldn't blame her for being mad. It was very insulting to her family. My sister, Sammie, was standing right next to her.

"At least Candido and Esperanza do honest work and don't hurt anyone," Sammie chimed in. Then, glancing over at Sean and Jared, she added, "Can you say the same thing about those jerks over there?"

Sammie is not at all intimidated by the SF2 girls or by the rich members of the club. She says what she wants, no matter what anyone thinks. That's why she and those Truth Teller friends of hers get along so well. They call it speaking from the heart. I love my sister, but sometimes I wish her heart would not have so much to say.

Bethany focused her eyes on Sammie. "I take it you're the other sister," she said. "The pudgy one with the sassy mouth."

"You mean the one who tells it like it is," Alicia said.

"And proud of it," Sammie added.

I closed my eyes and made a wish.

Please, Sammie. Don't go into your Truth Teller speech. Not here. Not now. In fact, not ever.

She probably would have, but I was saved by the arrival of Dennis and Carol Ann Wadsworth.

"Oh look," Bethany said as the white picket gate

from the parking lot opened up. "Finally. Hi, Mom! Hi, Daddy! Over here."

Bethany's mom and dad waved and made their way across the deck over to us.

Mrs. Wadsworth was what GoGo likes to call "a handsome woman," meaning she wasn't pretty in a frilly kind of way but in a sleek "I-only-wear-black" kind of way. She was dressed in black pants and a black silk top that matched her shiny black hair. Not exactly what you'd call a beach look. Her husband, on the other hand, had on the ultimate in beach wear—he was decked out in powder-blue shorts with flip-flops to match, and a pink polo shirt, collar popped, naturally. He had a nice smile, though, so I forgave him for the collar look.

"Hi, girls," Mrs. Wadsworth said when she reached us. She seemed unaware of the tension in the air. Holding out her hand to me, she said, "I'm Carol Ann Wadsworth. I don't believe we've met. You must be new to the club."

"Oh no—" I began, but was cut off by Mr. Wadsworth.

"How about that, Carol Ann," he said. "We go to Spain for the summer and come back to a whole new membership."

"I'm Charlie Diamond," I persisted, "and this is my twin sister, Sammie. We're not actually members."

I wanted to set the record straight before this got any more embarrassing.

"Diamond? Oh, yes . . ." Mrs. Wadsworth said with a nod. "The children of the new tennis pro. Well, it's nice to meet you, anyway."

As she shook my hand, I felt her diamond rings crunching up against my fingers.

"Oh, and hello Alicia," she said. "Or now that we've summered in Spain, perhaps I should say, *buenos días, señorita.*"

"That's okay, Mrs. Wadsworth." I could tell Alicia was annoyed. "I've lived in America since I was three. I speak English."

"Oh I know, darling, but don't you find it such *fun* to speak Spanish?"

I could see that Alicia's mouth was twitching slightly, like she had words right behind her lips that were bursting to come out. I knew that at any second, she could snap and point out that her family didn't speak Spanish for fun but because it's the language that people who come from El Salvador actually speak. Mrs. Wadsworth didn't seem aware that there was any problem with Alicia. She just smiled and threw one of her tan arms around Lauren.

"So, my darling niece, Bethany said she was going to give you a little initiation assignment today," she said. "How'd it go?"

"Mom, it was so hilarious," Bethany answered for Lauren. "Lauren had to walk and cluck like a chicken until I said she could stop."

To my surprise, Mrs. Wadsworth threw back her

head and laughed, too. If it had been my mother, she would have given me a lecture about being nice to other people and not giving in to peer pressure. But Mrs. Wadsworth just said, "You know, girls, I was a Wave, too, back in the day. For my initiation, I had to wear all my clothes inside out for a week. It was so embarrassing, but that's half the fun of initiation, don't you think, Charlie?"

Before I could open my mouth, Lauren answered for me.

"Charlie wouldn't know," she snapped, "because she's not going to be initiated."

"What's the matter?" Mr. Wadsworth asked me. "You're not interested in joining the Junior Waves? It's lots of fun and a good way to meet football players. That's how Carol Ann and I met."

"Daddy, you don't understand," Bethany said. "It's not going to be a club that's open to just anyone."

"It's going to be open only to my friends," Lauren added. She looked at me with a raised eyebrow and her look made it clear that did not mean me.

"None of us would want to join your club, anyway," Sammie interrupted. "We have better things to do with our time than sit around and make up cheers."

I wished Sammie would speak for herself. I loved the idea of being in the Junior Waves. It sounded totally cool.

"Besides," Sammie went on, as if she hadn't done enough damage already. "You guys don't even know if you're going to get permission to start a club at Beachside. You're only allowed to start an afterschool club if your grades are good, you know."

I could see that Lauren looked very surprised by this.

"You never mentioned grades," she whispered to Bethany.

"I'm sure you guys all do fine," Bethany answered. "It's easy to get good grades in middle school. Wait until you get to the hard stuff in high school, like chemistry and trig-o-whatever-it-is."

"Trigonometry, honey," her father said.

"If you say so, Daddy."

Lauren looked a little worried. I happen to know that her grades are not that good. And as for the other girls in the SF2s: Lily March was a good student, but Jillian Kendall and Brooke Addison were not exactly on the honor roll. In fact, pretty much the opposite. Jillian's main source of information is reality television, and Brooke, well, let's just say that if they gave out As for getting tan, she'd be a straight-A student. As far as other subjects go, she's pretty marginal.

The screen door to the clubhouse slammed and we all turned around to see GoGo limping out.

"You must be Dennis and Carol Ann," she said. "I heard you pull up. Bethany and I have had quite a planning session for her party. Why don't we all go into the kitchen and talk food? It's one of my favorite topics."

She took Bethany by the arm and as she started to guide her toward the kitchen, she turned to Sammie.

"You and Alicia should come into the living room. I believe Lauren and Charlie have a lot to talk over, and they might want a little privacy."

She flashed me a look, but I knew that even if Lauren I were left alone, it would do no good. She had made it very clear that our friendship was over.

"I was hoping that you and I could talk this whole thing through, Lauren," I said giving it a last desperate shot. "We were too close to just let our friendship die."

Did her expression soften? I wasn't sure.

But before she could say anything, the gate from the parking lot swung open, and Jillian, Brooke, and Lily walked up, laughing like they had just heard the funniest joke in the world.

"Hey, Lauren!" Jillian yelled. "Come check out what Lily's got on. Another fabulous outfit that only Miss Style could pull off."

Lily was wearing red cowboy boots and jean shorts and as always, she looked so original. She just has a way with clothes, and we all know she's going to be a fashion designer when she grows up. Or before.

Lauren nodded in my direction, and the others followed her gaze. When they saw me, Jillian and Brooke suddenly stopped laughing. Only Lily March said something.

"Hi, Charlie," she said, "It's nice to see you."

"Oh really?" Brooke said. "Maybe it is for you, Lily, but not so much for me."

My cheeks started to burn. "Lauren and I were just having a talk," I managed to say.

"Looks like you guys were in the middle of a major heart-to-heart," Jillian said. "Like the one I saw on *Teen Super Models* last night where Tori told Ella that she was going to own the runway and then Ella tells Tori that she was nothing but a runway hog and everybody knew she only got the cover of *Teen Vogue* because her dad's a famous fashion photographer."

"Actually, Charlie and I are done talking," Lauren declared.

Then turning to me, she said, "If you'll excuse us, we have to get to work on our Junior Waves application. So maybe you can, like, go somewhere else?"

That stung.

I went inside. On the couch, Sammie and Alicia were looking over a bunch of ocean crud.

"This rock is smooth on one side, but jagged on the other," Sammie was saying. "Like the way our feelings are tumbled smooth by the waves of life but still some areas remain jagged."

Oh brother. Sammie and I may be identical on the outside, but we sure weren't on the inside.

I pressed my face against the window and saw Lauren sitting at the table with the other girls. She had the application in front of her, and they were all talking at the same time while she filled it out.

It was just another Saturday at the Sporty Forty Beach Club. Everyone had something to do, someone to be with.

Everyone but me.

An Invitation

....

Chapter 3

"Tournament day," Sammie said the next morning, shaking my shoulder to wake me up. "As Dad would say, '*Up and at 'em.*'"

I yawned and stretched in bed. It was weird having Sammie be the one who was up first. Usually, she's the one who never wants to get out of bed.

"So what do we think, Charlie?" She pulled my tennis outfit out of the drawer and tossed it on the bed. "Are you going to play another match of who-cares tennis, or is today the day you're going to perk up and show a little fight?"

She was right. For the past few weeks, I had been playing the worst tennis of my life. I have to admit, part of the fun of playing competitive tennis is the respect it brings from the people around you.

"Wow, Sammie and Charlie just got ranked tenth in California," people say. Or *"Charlie served eleven aces in that match. The girl's a star."* It feels good to hear that. But when the SF2s kicked me out, all their praise for my tennis evaporated, too. Ever since, it's been hard to get motivated. At our tournament last weekend, Alicia and her friend Sara Berlin showed up to root for Sammie, but no one was in the stands rooting for me. Not one friend.

"Our first match is at ten," Sammie told me. "We're up against Fritz and Fernandez from the San Diego Racquet Club. They're supposed to be monsters." She made her orangutan face and stalked around our room like a monster, faking serves and growling like a beast. I just rolled over in bed.

"Come on, Charles. Dad's out there cutting up a million orange slices and loading the car with giant water bottles. We're going to be so hydrated, we may have to play the match in the girl's bathroom."

She laughed and looked over at me, hoping I would join in.

"Could you maybe crack a little smile?" she coaxed. "I'm working hard here to cheer you up."

Being my identical twin, Sammie always knows what I'm feeling. I knew she could feel my sadness, almost as if she were experiencing it herself. I'm the same way with her. So even though she's never been a fan of the SF2s, she knew how much I had wanted to be part of their group, and instinctively felt bad for me. I appreciated her efforts to lift my spirits, I really did, so I managed a weak little smile.

"Wow," she said. "Is that the best you can do?"

I nodded. She reached down and gave me a Sammie hug. I don't know how to describe it exactly, but let's just say it's big and long. When Sammie hugs you, you definitely know you've been hugged.

"I wish I could fix things for you, Charles," she said.

"You and me both."

"Well, since I can't, you have no choice but to get up and face the day. I don't want to have to carry you out to the car. Even sisters have their limits, you know."

I got dressed in the same outfit that Sammie was wearing. We never dress alike, except when we're playing doubles. Dad says it throws off the opposition to see two more-or-less identical people on the other side of the court. Makes them think they're seeing double.

We got our gear together and walked into the living room, where our Dad was jangling the car keys in one hand and holding the largest plastic bag of orange slices you've ever seen in the other. It could have hydrated all of Australia.

"Come on, girls," he said. "GoGo's already in the car with Alicia and Sara."

"Oh, I didn't know your friends were coming," I said to Sammie.

"I couldn't stop them. They wanted to be there to

support me. Uh, I mean *us*."

Alicia is the sweetest person in the world, but I have to confess, I don't exactly get Sara Berlin. She's really tall and has a huge head of curly hair that sticks out like a lion's mane. Sammie says she's earthy, but to me, she always looks like she's just come back from living in a hut somewhere in the Amazon. Like, she wears jewelry made of sea shells, and peasant shirts with puffy sleeves, and the only kind of shoes she wears are sandals or boots, nothing in between. Today she was wearing black lace-up boots with a long flowered skirt that looked like it used to be couch pillows.

Wow, I thought to myself. She is really going to stand out at the Sand and Surf Tennis Club where the tournament was being held. It's a very straitlaced place about two miles up the coast from us. Most of their members wear some combination of navy blue and white. The only couch-pillow material you see there is on the couches. But since Sara was being nice enough to come and watch us play, I felt it was my duty to be nice to her.

"Cool boots, Sara," I said as I wiggled into the backseat next to her. "Thanks for coming."

"Yeah, it's so great to have supportive friends," Sammie said as she climbed into the way back.

My dad started the car. "Just don't let the presence of your friends distract you girls," he warned. "You're participating in this tournament to win, not to socialize."

And win we did, but just barely. We finally beat Fritz and Fernandez in a tiebreaker that seemed to go on forever. Sammie played strong and steady, and it was her consistency that got us to the tiebreaker. But it was me who hit the two winning shots—a passing shot that whizzed right by Hailey Fritz, and a match-ending drop shot that Eva Fernandez couldn't get her racket on. I have to confess, it felt great to win. I had been feeling like such a loser lately, so the rush of emotions that came with that victory was thrilling.

After the match, Sammie threw her arm around my shoulder and said, "That's the old Charlie. Way to go. We'll have to go out for our victory pizza later."

We had actually skipped our last victory pizza dinner, a tradition we've been observing since we were ten. It was my fault. I didn't go because I had plans with the SF2s.

"One large sausage and mushroom and two Vanilla Cokes, coming right up." I smiled.

"Yup. The mighty Diamond twosome is back," she said, and that felt good.

The whole group stopped at Chilly's Frozen Yogurt on the way home, and everyone was in a great mood. I was feeling so loose, I even got the large cup of chocolate-vanilla swirl and loaded on the rainbow sprinkles and white chocolate chips, something I would never have done with my SF2 friends. They all get a small cup of low-fat vanilla with no toppings because it only has 150 calories.

When we arrived back at the Sporty Forty parking lot, Dad and GoGo went into the club while Alicia and Sara helped Sammie and me get our gear from the car. Sara was telling this really funny story about a time she slow danced with Will Lee, a boy so short he only comes up to the bottom of her boobs. When they were dancing, he didn't know if he should look up, look down, or look straight into them. There was something about the phrase "bottom of my boobs" that sent us all into a fit of laughter.

We were still giggling when we pushed open the gate and entered the club. Sitting there at the table closest to us was Ryan, his laptop open in front of him. He was surrounded by Lauren, Jillian, and Brooke, who were looking unhappily at a pile of papers in front of them.

I immediately felt embarrassed to be seen having such a good time with Alicia and Sara. All I could think about was that Alicia was the daughter of the groundskeeper and that Sara was wearing a skirt that looked like a couch pillow. Would Lauren and the other girls think that I had given up wanting to be an SF2 and had suddenly joined the Geek Patrol?

I know it wasn't the nicest thought in the world, but it's the truth.

"We were just at a t-tennis tournament," I stammered, as though that explained why I was hanging out with these girls.

"I know," Lauren said, barely looking up from her papers.

"Wow, word travels fast. Who told you?"

Lauren put her arm on Ryan's.

"Your dad called Ryan to say you guys won. And you know Ryan, he tells me *everything*. We're so close."

"You are? Does Ryan know that?" Sammie asked, an edge in her voice.

"As a matter of fact, he does," Lauren snapped. "Which is why he volunteered to help us fill out our application for Junior Waves. He wouldn't do that for just anyone. Isn't that right, Ryan?"

"Well, I wouldn't exactly call it volunteering," Ryan explained. "But watching these girls try to fill out the form was driving me nuts, so Captain Ry-Guy and his trusty laptop stepped in to save the day."

Lauren laughed like Ryan had just said the funniest thing in the world.

"Your brother is so totally hysterical," she said. Ryan looked pretty pleased with the compliment and Lauren shot me a look that practically said, "See, I told you he has a crush on me."

"Well, I need to use the computer after lunch to work on my history paper," Sammie said. "So how long is this application thing going to take?"

"Maybe forever," Jillian groaned. "They want to know everything about us. Not just our grades, but our extracurricular activities, and community service, and hobbies, and awards and honors."

"I do a ton of community service," Brooke said. "Just the other day, I gave a little kid on the beach my sunscreen because his shoulders were getting all red."

"I think they mean real community service," Alicia said. "Like, I work at the food bank, and Sammie tutors a first-grader, and Charlie cleans up litter on the beach."

"*Eeuuwww,*" Brooke said, wrinkling her nose at me. "You mean touch other people's trash? That's not sanitary."

"I wear rubber gloves," I said, which only made her say "*Eeuuwww*" even louder.

"Well, I was just telling Ryan that I have an honor that would really impress the principal," Jillian said. "I auditioned for *Teen Super Model,* and the producer said she'd call me if I got the part."

"Did she call?" Sara asked her.

"Not yet. It's only been six months. They could still call."

"Good luck with that one," Sammie snickered.

"Ease up, Sam-I-Am," Ryan said. "You can't blame the girls for trying to come up with things that sound good on the application. Not all of us are like you and Charlie, who can get good grades and be tennis champs at the same time."

As he said that, I noticed that Lauren took her legs off the table and sat straight up in her chair. She turned and looked at me, as if she were just seeing me for the first time. I smiled at her, and then I noticed that Sammie was watching Lauren carefully. She was squinting, the way she does when she sees something she doesn't like.

"Come on, guys," she said to Alicia and Sara. "Let's go inside. GoGo said she'd make up a bowl of guacamole and chips."

"Did someone say guacamole?" Ryan said, jumping to his feet. "I'm there."

He leaped out of his chair and sprinted toward the kitchen.

"But what about our application?" Jillian called after him.

"Guacamole first. Chips second. Application third," he called back to them. "I'll be back. You girls talk among yourselves."

Knowing that I wasn't welcome to hang out with them, I turned to follow Ryan and Sammie into the kitchen. I hadn't even taken two steps, when I heard Lauren say.

"Hey, Charlie, can you hang back for a few minutes?" Lauren asked. "We want to talk to you."

I felt my heart leap.

"Sure," I said.

Sammie stopped and took me by the arm.

"Don't do it, Charles," she whispered, shaking her head. "You know what they're after."

"I don't know what you're talking about," I whispered back. "Listen, you guys go inside. I'll join you in a few minutes."

As soon as they left, I dropped my tennis bag and pulled one of the red cushioned deck chairs up to the table.

"We've missed you," Lauren said, putting her hand on my arm.

"We have?" Jillian asked.

"Jills, let me talk," Lauren said to her. Lauren is in charge of the SF2s, and when she talks, everyone listens. Turning back to me, she went on. "I was just about to say to the girls that we should ask you to come back to the group."

"Really?"

"Uh-huh. As we were filling out this application, I was thinking how cool it would be if you were in the Junior Waves, too. You know, all of us together."

"I'd give anything to be a Junior Wave, Lauren. It sounds so fun."

"We're going to get to go to the Friday night football games at the high school and sit with the real Waves," Jillian said.

"Once I sat in the high-school section at a basketball game," Brooke added, "but I only got to because the General's brother is on the team and he snuck us in. Everyone there thought I was really in high school. It was the best."

The General is Brooke's boyfriend, and if I do say so myself, they make a great-looking couple. Of course, his real name isn't the General, but everyone calls him that because he always wears camouflage cargo pants to school. It's his look. Her look is blonde, tan, and gorgeous.

"Who else are you asking to be in the Junior Waves?" I asked.

"Me, Brooke, Lauren, Lily, and you," Jillian said.

"What about the guys?" I asked.

"At the high school, most of The Waves are girls," Brooke answered, "except for a few weird dudes. I don't think Ben Feldman or Spencer want to be Junior Waves. And I one hundred percent know that the General would say no."

"And we can't even ask Jared and Sean," Jillian said. "Since they're on probation, they're not allowed to do anything . . . after . . . well . . . you know."

She looked at me, and I lowered my eyes, shifting uncomfortably in my chair. Was I ever going to stop getting blamed for what happened to them?

"Listen, girls, let's not get into that again," Lauren said. "There's no point in holding a grudge, is there, Charlie?"

"No, there isn't. I've been hoping you would come to see it that way."

"Well, the point is, I think you'd make a good addition to the Junior Waves. Do you want to be included on the application? If you say yes, Charlie, we'll put everything that happened behind us and go back to being friends."

I couldn't believe it. It was perfect. This is just the way the conversation between us had happened in my imagination the day before. But before I could answer, Ryan came galloping back from the kitchen, a plastic cup of orange juice in his hands.

"Nothing like GoGo's guacamole followed by a cool OJ," he said. "Best snack in the world."

He went to leap over the back of his chair, but one of his flip-flops got caught and he stumbled. The orange juice flew out of the cup and spilled all over Lauren.

"Oh no," she squealed, jumping up and trying to shake it off of her white T-shirt.

"Oops," Ryan said. "I guess I underestimated the size of my feet. Sorry."

Lauren put her hands up to her head.

"Did it get in my hair, Charlie?"

"A little. I'll go inside and get you a dish towel."

"Thanks. I don't want my hair to be all sticky and gross."

I dashed into the kitchen. GoGo was putting the dishes in the dishwasher. Sammie, Alicia, and Sara were sitting on stools at the counter.

"I need some towels," I said, heading for the drawer under the sink. "For Lauren."

"What'd she do?" Sammie asked. "Smudge her eye makeup?"

I opened the drawer and took out a couple of clean towels.

"Charlie," Sammie said. "They asked you to join the Junior Waves, didn't they? I just know it."

"So what if they did?" I answered. There was irritation in my voice.

"Don't you see? They only want you so you'll make their application look good. Aside from Lily March, none of those girls have decent grades, or have ever done any community service. Your grades and our tennis titles will help them qualify. That's why they're asking you."

"That's not true," I snapped. "You don't know everything."

"Principal Pfeiffer just turned down an application from our friend Etta to start an Electronic Dance Music Club," Alicia said. "He said she had to prove that she could improve her grades and participate in other extracurriculars, too. Otherwise, starting a club could be too distracting."

"I have to go," I said.

"Just think it over before you agree," Sammie begged.

Suddenly, I felt like I was going to explode. And I did.

"They're my friends, Sammie!" I yelled, surprising myself at how much emotion came pouring out all at once. "Don't you see? I don't have any other friends!"

My eyes filled with tears.

"You have us," Sara said. "Come with us to Truth Tellers. You'll find a lot of friends there. Everyone is very accepting."

"We're having our regular meeting tomorrow after school," Alicia said. "Just come and see what it's like. You'll be surprised how much fun it is."

"And we don't want you for your credentials," Sammie said. "We want you just because you're you."

It was a sweet offer, it really was. At the same time, though, I knew that deep down I was not a Truth Teller type.

I looked over at GoGo for advice. She had stopped dishing out the chips and was listening carefully.

"What do you think I should do?" I asked her.

She just shook her head.

"I can't make these decisions for you. That's what growing up is all about. Sometimes you make the right decision. Sometimes you make the wrong one. You learn from both."

That was no help. Clearly, I was on my own.

I grabbed the towels and headed out to the deck, letting the door slam behind me.

The Secret

....

Chapter 4

"Welcome, Truth Tellers, one and all," Ms. Carew said. "Please gather in our acceptance circle."

It was the next day and I was standing at the door of Ms. Carew's room. She's my English teacher, but also the sponsor of Truth Tellers, which meets every Monday at three fifteen. Sammie and Alicia and Sara were already inside, hanging out with about ten other members of the club. I had arrived five minutes earlier but just couldn't get myself to step over the threshold into the room.

I had stayed up late discussing my situation with GoGo. She knew that Sammie wanted me to reject the SF2s and join Truth Tellers. GoGo told me that it was my decision who my friends should be, and no one else's. When I went upstairs to get ready for bed, Sammie kept hammering me with her view that the SF2s were using me to get what they wanted. She wouldn't quit.

In desperation, I called my mom in Boston. She suggested that I try going to Truth Tellers with Sammie and then decide how I was feeling. So, I promised Sammie that I would try it, that I would be open and accepting. But already I could feel myself closing up at the thought of entering the room.

Ms. Carew walked over to the doorway.

"Charlie, are you coming in?" she asked. "You are more than welcome, but I need to close the door for privacy."

That sounded like an easy enough question. *Are you coming in or staying out? Yes or no.* But I didn't answer. What was my problem?

I hadn't told anyone except Sammie that I was going. I certainly didn't mention it to Lauren. All I told her was that I had to ask my dad if it was okay to join the Junior Waves and that I would let her know today. At lunch, I went to the one place you'll never run into Lauren: the library. When I saw her in PE, she asked if we could meet at the Sporty Forty after school and work on the application. I told her I had a dentist appointment.

"Charlie?" I heard Ms. Carew saying. "Are you in or out?"

"I'm in," I said, stepping into the room and shutting the door. "At least, for now."

"That's fine," she said. "We all welcome you. Come be part of our acceptance circle."

The chairs in Ms. Carew's classroom had been pushed back against the wall so there was room for everyone to stand in a big circle. They joined hands and started to hum. I stood between Will Lee and a girl named Etta, who had spiky green tips on her short black hair. Will gave me a big smile as he took my hand. His hand was pretty clammy.

"You're very attractive," he whispered.

"You're only in sixth grade. You shouldn't say stuff like that."

"Why not? It's what I feel."

He might have winked at me, but I'm not totally sure because I quickly turned away and focused my eyes on Sammie, who was standing between Alicia and a redheaded boy named Bernard. Everyone, except me, was humming.

"We hum to get used to hearing the sound of our own voices," Ms. Carew explained, as if she could sense my confusion. "The human voice is powerful when it speaks the truth. More powerful than any weapon in the world."

I gave the humming a shot. I wasn't sure what song I was supposed to hum so I did a little version of "Happy Birthday" until I realized that I was the only one humming a song. Everyone else was just humming a single note.

After we were all hummed out, Ms. Carew gave an

introduction to the meeting.

"We welcome everyone here into our acceptance circle," she said, "where each of us is free to be exactly who we are and know that no one will judge us. In this circle, in this room, we are free to speak our truths without fear."

I had to admit, that sounded pretty good.

"The subject today is Secrets," Ms. Carew said. "Who here has a secret?"

Everyone's hand shot up into the air, including mine. She looked over at me and smiled.

"Sometimes we keep secrets because we want privacy; that is, we want to keep something all to ourselves. And that's fine," she said. "But there are other kinds of secrets we keep out of fear. We are afraid to show this part of ourselves, for fear we'll be made fun of or appear to be different. What I have learned," she went on, "is that when we share these kinds of secrets, we find out that we are not that different from one another. Deep down, we're all afraid of—and want—the same things."

Ms. Carew sat down on the floor cross-legged in her beautiful African-print skirt, and slipped off her sandals. As the rest of us sat down, I noticed that her toenails were painted the same lime green as my fingernails, which looked really beautiful against her brown skin. You don't often find a teacher with hot-green nail polish on her toes. From across the circle, Sammie watched me check out Ms. Carew's fashionable feet and flashed me an amused smile, as if to say, "*I told you she was cool.*"

"Today, I'd like to ask if anyone is willing to share a secret," Ms. Carew said. "Know that whatever we say in this room stays in this room, and that your secret is safe with us."

The first one to raise a hand was Bernard.

"I keep my weight a secret," he said, "because I weigh more than anyone thinks I do. I have this roll of fat around my middle that no one knows about. When I go to the beach, I keep my shirt on and when my family asks why, I tell them that I don't want to get sunburned. So I guess you could say that everything between my chest and my hips is a big fat secret."

I was amazed. First, because he was so willing to just put it out there. And second, because I never thought boys worried about their weight or how they looked in a bathing suit. It was news to me.

"I know exactly how you feel, Bernard," Sammie was saying. "I worry all the time about my weight. I'm always wondering if everyone is looking at me and thinking how fat I am."

"You're not fat," I responded immediately. "You look fine. Dad's just made you feel fat because you're heavier than me."

Ms. Carew held up her hand.

"Charlie," she said gently. "I know Sammie appreciates your remarks, but we're not here to talk people out of how they're feeling. Whatever they feel is their truth, and we have to listen with open hearts and accept their feelings as real."

That seemed crazy to me. I mean, just because you feel something doesn't make it true. But everyone else was nodding in agreement. Suddenly, I felt so stupid sitting there.

The next person to talk was Will Lee.

"My secret is that I like older women," he said. "I'm only in the sixth grade, but I'm always falling in love with seventh-graders."

Was he looking at me out of the corner of his eye? Oh no, I hoped not.

"Recently, I had a crush on one of my sister's friends, and she's in the eighth grade," he went on. "I asked if she wanted to hang out with me some weekend, and she rejected me. Made up some phony excuse about having a boyfriend, which I happen to know she doesn't because I hear her talking on the phone with my sister."

"You need to pick on people your own size." I chuckled, giving him a friendly little poke in the ribs. It was hard to take him seriously. He seemed like such a little kid.

"I'm uncomfortable with the way you're acting," a girl named Keisha said. I looked around to see who she was talking to—it was me!

"I was just making a joke," I said.

"Will was opening up about a secret he has," Keisha said. "I don't think he was looking to be laughed at."

I felt myself flush with anger.

"I wasn't laughing *at* him," I said in a voice that sounded snappier than I had intended. "I was laughing *with* him. There's a big difference."

"Charlie is new to our group," Ms. Carew told the others. "She's just learning to listen and accept."

Boy, that made me feel even more idiotic. How hard is it to listen? I have ears and Dr. Hartley checks my hearing every year at my annual checkup. I *was* listening. I truly didn't understand what I was doing wrong.

"I just want to support Charlie and say that I'm glad she's here," Alicia said. "She's been going through some tough times, and she could use all our support."

Everyone in the circle turned to me. I felt like they were expecting me to spill my guts about what I'd been going through, but I could feel myself closing up like a clam shell. I hate it when I'm expected to do something that I'm not comfortable doing. Like, when we were little, our Mom would always want Sammie and me to sing "Oh Susannah" at family gatherings so everyone would see how cute we were. I remember one year pretending to zip my mouth shut, refusing to open it for the whole party. Call me stubborn, but I don't perform like a trained dog.

"Do you feel like sharing with us, Charlie?" Ms. Carew said.

"Maybe some other time," was all I could muster.

"We're okay with that," she said. "It takes a while

to build up trust. Does anyone else want to share a secret? Take it out in the open and let it breathe."

Sara Berlin put her hand up tentatively.

"This is something I've never talked about to anyone except my mom," she began. "And it's going to be really hard to share. It's kind of similar to what Bernard was saying about being afraid to take his shirt off."

I wondered what it could be. It certainly couldn't be her weight. Sara was tall and slim, with not an extra ounce of fat on her.

"So Bernard was basically saying that he was ashamed of his body," she began. "I am, too."

"This is a very common theme we all share," Ms. Carew said. "No one's body is perfect, and yet we all feel that we have to keep our imperfections a secret."

"Is it about your hair?" a guy named Devon asked. "It's obviously really different than most girls' hair, but I think it's awesome the way it sticks out all over the place. It's like it's saying, 'I will not be ruled by you.' That's awesome."

"Well, it is about my hair, but then again, it's not," Sara said. Everyone just sat there quietly, while she actually wrung her hands with nervousness. Wow, why didn't she just spit it out? This hinting around at everything was driving me crazy. As far as I was concerned, it's either about your hair or it's not.

Sara took a deep breath and then suddenly reached up with both hands and pulled her hair up behind her ears. It was so thick and curly that when she pulled it all together on top of her head, it looked like a fluffy black cloud was hanging over her.

"See," she said. "There's my secret. Now it's out. Or I should say, *they're* out."

As I stared at her, I realized that I had never seen Sara with her hair up. Now that there was no hair surrounding her face, the thing you noticed were her ears. It's not like they were deformed or anything like that. But they were really big and stuck out far from her head. And when I say 'far from her head,' I mean *very* far from her head.

"Kids have been teasing me about my ears ever since I can remember," she said, tears welling up in her eyes. "Even when I was in preschool, one of the kids told me I looked like Dumbo."

Ms. Carew sighed. "Children can be cruel," she said. "That must have been very hard for you, Sara."

She nodded. When she spoke again, her voice sounded like she had that lump in your throat you get when you're trying really hard not to burst into tears.

"Ever since I realized I had protruding ears, I've covered them up with my hair. Thank goodness it's thick and curly. But I'm always afraid that on windy days, my hair's going to blow back and everyone will see what I really look like."

"Have you tried really strong hair spray?" I asked.

Bernard looked at me, put his finger to his lips, and said "Shhhh."

What was his problem? I was just trying to offer a helpful suggestion.

"Go on, Sara," Ms. Carew said.

"My parents know how much this has affected my self-esteem," she said. "And there is a surgery that can correct it. It's called otoplasty, and they actually operate and pin your ears back so they're closer to your head."

"Oh cool," I said. "Like an ear tuck. You should get that right away."

"Charlie," Ms. Carew said gently. "Please let Sara express herself without interrupting."

I wanted to tell her that I was just trying to be helpful.

"It's really expensive," Sara said. "At least five thousand dollars. And we don't have the money because my little brother is autistic and has to have a special tutor, which costs a lot, too. So I'm stuck looking like this, until I can earn enough to have the operation."

She let go of her hair and let it fall back down around her face. It was like a signal for everyone in the room to gather around her in a group hug. Everyone but me. I didn't want to be snuggling up with a bunch of people I barely knew.

"Thank you for sharing that with us, Sara," Ms. Carew said, joining in the hug. "We're all here for you. I think everyone understands the relief of getting your secrets out in the open."

Maybe everyone else in that room understood that, but I didn't. Why was she better off now that everyone knew she had protruding ears? It didn't help them look any better. It didn't help her earn the money to get them fixed. It didn't take away all the teasing she'd had to bear her whole life. As far as I was concerned, it just spread the misery around.

After Sara's story, the meeting kind of went downhill. A few other kids shared some minor secrets, but nothing that could compare with Sara's. Ms. Carew recited a poem by a guy named Keats that said that beauty is truth and truth is beauty. I didn't get it. To end the meeting, Ms. Carew put on some crazy flute music, and invited everyone to free dance, letting their bodies express their inner secrets. I was the only one who didn't accept the invitation.

"You're not dancing," Ms. Carew said when she saw me perch on one of the desks pushed against the wall.

"I need steps when I dance," I said. "And a beat doesn't hurt, either."

"I see. Well, maybe next time you'll feel like dancing. I hope you come back, Charlie."

"Thanks," I told her. "I probably will."

But a little voice inside me, the one that doesn't speak out loud, was saying just the opposite.

A Decision

....

Chapter 5

"I can't do it," I told Sammie on the walk home. "I can't be a Truth Teller. It's just not me."

"Sure you can," she protested. "Everyone loved you."

"First of all, they didn't love me. Every time I opened my mouth, I got weird looks from people. I don't blame them. In that room, with that group, I am weird. I don't fit in."

"But didn't you feel how powerful the group was? Like when Sara described her awful ear problem. It was just so honest and raw."

"I feel sorry for her, I really do. She's a nice girl and I'm glad she's one of your best friends. But that doesn't mean she has to be my best friend."

"Okay, we can talk about this more over our

pizza at dinner tonight," Sammie said. "Dad said he'd take us to Barone's, and he's even agreed to pay for it. Apparently, yesterday's match moved us up in the rankings so he's in a generous mood."

Sammie and I paused at the red light on the corner of Pacific Coast Highway. Traffic was backed up with people headed to the beach to watch the sunset. There's this public parking lot right next to the club and at four o'clock, they open the gates and let everyone in for free. People either sit in their cars and watch the sun go down, or get out and walk along the beach, waiting for that exact moment when the sun flattens out and disappears into the Pacific. Before dinner, Sammie and I usually go down to the beach with GoGo and watch the sunset. GoGo says any time you have a chance to watch the sun set over the ocean, you should not miss it. I think that's pretty good advice.

I was glad for the heavy traffic because the roar of the cars whizzing by made it hard to talk or be heard. I was tired of talking. Sammie and I were never going to agree, and I was tired of her trying to convince me to love her friends. You can't make yourself love people you don't love.

And speaking of love, when we crossed the street and pushed open the gate to the Sporty Forty, who should we find sitting on the deck but Spencer Ballard. Apart from being the cutest boy I know, with dimples the size of the Grand Canyon, he is also the only boy I've ever kissed. Okay, it was just one kiss one night on the beach. That was before everything blew up between me and the SF2s, and he's kept some distance between us since then. He's nice and polite and everything when he sees me, but he's definitely acted awkward the few times we've been alone together since then. I can understand that he's not sure how to act around me anymore. It just sucks.

"Hey," he said when he saw us. "You guys always get home this late from school?"

"Oh, we were at a Truth Tellers meeting," Sammie blurted out. I wanted to stuff a sock in her mouth.

"Sammie was at the meeting," I hurried to explain. "I was just checking it out."

"I'm trying to get Charlie to join," Sammie said. "She could use some better friends, if you know what I mean."

I thought Spencer would hate her saying that. But he just nodded and gave me one of those smiles where his dimples light up his face like stars in the sky.

"The group has been pretty rough on you," he acknowledged. "I keep telling them they haven't been fair, that they need to see things from your point of view, too."

If I hadn't been so tongue-tied, I swear I would have asked him to marry me right there on the spot. I know twelve is too young to get married, but at least we could get engaged.

"But Lauren says that maybe you're going to join

some club she's starting," he added. "So that's a good sign."

"That's what she thinks," Sammie said. "Charlie and I have other ideas." She seemed prepared to go on about it, but lucky for me, she was interrupted by GoGo yelling from the kitchen.

"Quesadillas just out of the pan," she called. "Any takers?"

And before you could say *salsa verde,* Sammie had dropped her backpack and dashed into the clubhouse.

"So what exactly did Lauren tell you?" I asked Spencer when she was out of sight.

"Only that she's invited you back into the group. I said that would be cool. For me, at least."

I felt myself melting and it wasn't from the sun. I looked down, trying to come up with just the right words to tell him that I had missed him. I didn't want to be overly gushy like the Truth Tellers, but I didn't want to be too distant and cool, either. As I turned some possible responses over in my mind, my dad came jogging off of the tennis court, a towel around his neck and his racket in his hand. It was so like him to pick the worst moment to show up on the scene.

"Spencer," he called out. "I just finished your mom's lesson. She wants you to play a couple games with her. Apparently, I didn't tucker her out enough."

"Guess I gotta go," Spencer said with a shrug. "I'll see you around, Charlie."

He stood up and walked off toward the tennis

courts, looking all golden in the setting sun. My dad flopped down in his seat.

"Thanks a lot, Dad," I said.

"For what?" he replied cluelessly. He popped the top off a bottle of Gatorade and dabbed his forehead with his towel. "Mrs. Ballard has a nice forehand. Nice level stroke. Actually, I think she's got much more potential than Mr. Ballard. Don't tell him that, though."

Tennis, tennis, tennis. Did he ever talk about anything else? Well, as a matter of fact, he did, right at that very moment.

"Lauren called," he said, taking a swig of Gatorade. "Three times."

"You didn't tell her where I was, did you?"

"I told her you were with Sammie. She was really eager to talk to you. In fact, she asked if I had made a decision yet. Is there something you haven't told me?"

If I had ever doubted whether or not I wanted to go back to the SF2s, my conversation with Spencer had put everything back in perspective. There was no decision to be made. What I wanted was crystal clear to me.

"Lauren and the girls are applying to start a Junior Waves club at school," I said. "They want me to be part of it. And I totally want to do it."

He nodded.

"So tell me, how much of your time do you think this club will take up? Because you know my feeling . . . school and tennis take priority over social activities."

Of course, I knew he was going to say that. It's his standard response whenever either of us asks to do anything. I pulled out my ready-made speech.

"I'm getting all As in school, Dad, except for maybe a B in Spanish, but I can bring that up if I practice with Esperanza and Alicia. And tennis-wise, Sammie and I are on a roll. You saw me finish off Fritz and Fernandez yesterday."

He nodded again. That was a good sign. I was so glad I had pulled it together for the tiebreaker.

"Well, I like the idea of you being part of a sports fan club," he said. "That makes a lot more sense than that wacky stuff your sister is into."

That was a typical comment. My dad thinks anything that isn't sports related is wacky.

"So I can do it?" I asked.

"School and tennis first. Do we understand each other?"

I nodded so vigorously that my head was in danger of toppling off my neck. He reached out and tousled my hair. "Okay, go call Lauren; she's waiting to hear from you."

"Thank you a million, billion times, Dad," I said, throwing my arms around his neck. "I won't let you down. I promise."

I practically flew into the kitchen. Inside, Sammie and GoGo were sitting at the counter, sampling several different kinds of quesadillas from a serving platter.

"Hey, Noodle," GoGo called. "Come have a taste. I'm trying to decide which one to serve as appetizers at Bethany's party. It's down to chicken and cheese or veggie with avocado."

"I'll be right back, GoGo. I've got to do something first."

I ran into my room and closed the door, grabbed my phone, and called Lauren.

"My dad said yes," I said without even so much as a hello. "I'm in!"

"Oh, Charlie, this is super awesome!" I heard her whisper "She's going to do it," to someone else in the room. In the background, I heard Jillian and Brooke cheer and echo Lauren's "this is super awesome" comment. Everyone in the SF2s, especially the girls, winds up talking like Lauren. She's the kind of person you want to be like.

Jillian grabbed the phone from Lauren.

"Can we come to the club right now and do the application?" she said. "The sooner we get it in, the sooner we'll know."

The last thing I wanted was for us to be sitting around working on the application with Sammie hovering nearby. It was going to be hard enough to tell her my decision, and I didn't need a constant stream of critical remarks from her.

"Would it be okay if I came to Lauren's instead?" I asked.

"Let me check." Then I heard Jillian whisper, "She

wants to come here." Lauren whispered something back to her, but I couldn't hear what she said.

"Lauren wants to know if Ryan is there at the club."

"No, he's at a volleyball team dinner."

I heard her whisper that to Lauren and then I overheard Lauren say, "In that case, tell her to come here."

"Lauren says it's great if you come here. We'll get the papers ready and order pizzas."

I ripped off my school clothes and put on my new hot-pink tank top and matching ballet flats I had been saving for a special occasion. Then I went back to the living room and slid onto the stool at the counter next to Sammie. Just by looking at what I was wearing, she knew what was up.

"They got you, didn't they?" she said.

I didn't answer, just reached out and took a bite of each of the quesadillas. Sammie talked while I chewed.

"You're not seeing things clearly, Charlie," she said. "I'm trying to protect you. These girls are using you. The last thing I want is for you to get hurt."

"I vote for the veggie with avocado," I said. "And Sams, I don't need your protection. I am old enough and smart enough to make my own decisions about my own friends."

"Charlie has proven that she can use good judgment," GoGo said. That shut Sammie up. Then turning to me, GoGo added, "Follow your instincts, and if it turns out you've made a mistake, learn from it. That's all we can do in life."

"Thanks, GoGo. See you guys in a little bit."

I slid off the stool and ran outside to find my Dad.

"Can you drop me at Lauren's house?" I asked.

"Well, that didn't take long," he answered. "Can this wait until after dinner? I thought you and Sammie were going out for your pizza celebration."

Oops. In the excitement of everything, I had totally forgotten about our plans. "I can't tonight. The girls have already ordered pizza for us," I explained.

"Did you tell Sammie your date is off?"

"She'll understand, Dad! Besides, she's already eaten a ton of quesadillas and she's probably full. We'll go to Barone's tomorrow. I know she'll be fine with that."

"Maybe you should talk to her first."

"I can't, Dad. I don't have time. Everyone is waiting for me."

"All right. I guess that's between the two of you, anyway. I'll get my keys."

Lauren lives in a huge house in the Palisades, overlooking the ocean. It's only a few minutes away, but the ride there seemed to take forever. It's strange how that is . . . when you want something to happen really fast, time seems to slow down just to torture you. Finally, we pulled into the circular driveway of Lauren's house. There's a fountain in the middle with a statue of a little boy peeing. We all think it's gross, but Lauren's mom says every elegant Italian mansion has one. I hopped out almost before my dad stopped the car.

"Don't bother saying good-bye," he called out as I ran to their huge front door with the stained glass windows and rang the bell.

From inside, I heard a ton of footsteps thundering down the stairs. The door flew open, and Lauren, Brooke, Jillian, and Lily were all there, holding out their arms to me.

I couldn't have asked for anything better.

The Application

....

Chapter 6

"Okay, let's get rid of these pizza boxes so we don't have cheese stains all over our application," Lauren said after dinner. "Esperanza! Could you please come here and take these?"

Alicia's mom, Esperanza, works at the Wadsworth's house when she's not working at the Sporty Forty. I think she spends three days at each job. I love Espie—she's become a great friend of our family and really helped take care of GoGo after she broke her leg. The last thing I wanted was for her to have to come into the kitchen to clean up our mess.

"I'll take care of this," I said, popping up and clearing the boxes off the table. "Where do you keep your recycling bin?"

"Oh, Charlie, you're such a hopelessly good girl," Lauren said.

"But that's what we love about you," Lily added.

By the time I had returned from dumping the boxes in the garbage bin, which was already out at the curb waiting for the next day's pick up, the papers were spread out on the table.

"So, Ryan already helped us enter most of this information on the application form," Lauren said, as I pulled up a chair. "We just have to add your answers. Let's write them down for now, and I can get my dad to put it all in the computer later."

"I can do it," I said. "It's not hard."

"Why bother?" said Lauren. "It's so much easier to have my dad do it. So, here's the first question. List your most important extracurricular activities and why they matter to you."

I didn't have to give that one a second thought.

"Well, for sure mine is playing competitive doubles tennis with my sister. It's really important because we're hoping to win scholarships one day to pay for college."

"College," Brooke nodded approvingly. "They'll like that. It sounds so serious."

"In a boring kind of way," Jillian added.

"Plus, we just got a new ranking," I said proudly. "We're now eleventh in the state in the fourteen-and-under category. If we keep it up, we'll make it to the Top Ten Club."

"Oh yeah. That's what I'm talking about," Lauren said, writing as fast as her pen could go. "The principal is going to love that."

"Can we highlight that in yellow?" Jillian asked.

Lily laughed. "I don't think you have to, Jilly," she said. "It's pretty impressive as is. I'd say it stands out all on its own."

I was on a feel-good roll now, so I just went on.

"Also, every year on Christmas Day, our whole family goes to the mission downtown and helps serve turkey dinners to the homeless people. It's a tradition."

"Not us," Brooke said. "Our tradition is ripping open all the presents and trying everything on."

Lauren burst out laughing and threw her arm around Brooke. "Remember that year when everything your mom bought you was one size too small?"

Brooke started to chuckle and groan at the same time.

"Brookie didn't stop crying all day," Lauren laughed. "It was so pathetic."

"Then our families went skiing together the next day," Lily explained to me. "Brooke was in such a bad mood, she didn't even want to leave the condo. So I stayed back with Brooke. We spent the whole day drinking hot chocolate."

"Okay, everyone, no more reminiscing. We still have to add Charlie's info to this whole section on grades," she said, picking up her pen again.

"Let's not and say we did," Jillian said. We all

cracked up. Lauren was done messing around, though.

"Charlie, what do you have for us?" she asked.

"Well, on my last report card, I got all As and one B."

"Unbelievable! That's exactly what I got!" Brooke giggled.

"Yeah, in your dreams," Lily said. "The day you get an A, I'll eat my hat." Then she took off the hat she was wearing, a cute black-and-red checkered one with actual earflaps, and pretended to be chomping it down. We all cracked up again.

It felt so good to be back with these girls. They knew each other so well that they just said and did whatever they felt like. It was like I had always known them.

It took us another hour to finish the application. We added some stuff about how I was new to Beachside Middle School and looking for an opportunity to participate in the community. And while we were making additions, we decided to put in a whole paragraph on Lily's talent for fashion design and how she had volunteered to make all the hats for Bethany's sweet sixteen. I suggested we put in that Lily was going to donate all the hats to a children's charity afterward, but Lauren didn't think Bethany would go for that.

Lauren decided that she and Lily would get to school early to turn in the application. If we all trooped in to Principal Pfeiffer's office together, it would look too much like we were a clique and not a school club. Lauren's very smart about these things.

"Let's all meet at our table at lunch to see if there's any news," Lauren said.

"Me too?" I asked, suddenly timid about whether I'd be welcome.

"Oh, I hadn't thought about that," Lauren said, pausing to consider what to do.

"Of course you too," Lily said, answering for Lauren. "You're back, remember?"

"But what about Jared and Sean? Won't they be there?" I asked.

"They're not the leaders of the SF2s," Lauren said. "You are definitely sitting at our lunch table. They'll just have to get used to that. We all will."

It had been such a big deal when the SF2s first invited me to sit with them at their table. They have the best table in the lunch pavilion, and every day the whole crowd gathers there to laugh and tell stories and make plans for what they'll do after school. I had really missed sitting with them the past three weeks. Once or twice, I'd had lunch with Sammie or Ryan, but mostly I just went to the library and ate lunch alone. The thought of joining them at "our" table again made me want to stand up and dance. Or at the very least, shave my legs.

Mrs. Wadsworth was on her way to meet some friends for a bridge game, so she offered to drive all of us home.

"Good luck to us," I said as I stood on the porch and said good-bye to Lauren. "Tomorrow's going to be a big day."

I was surprised when we all climbed into the backseat of the car to find Esperanza sitting in the front, next to Mrs. Wadsworth.

"*Hola, Charlito,*" she said. "Mrs. Wadsworth is driving me home, too. Did you have a nice time with your friends?"

I wanted to sink into the big black leather seat and disappear. I didn't want to seem like one of the rich girls in front of Esperanza. Usually, Espie and I talk about all kinds of things, and I practice my Spanish with her. But I didn't feel comfortable having our usual chat now that the other girls were in the car. We rode the rest of the way in silence.

When we pulled up in front of The Sporty Forty, I hopped out quickly. As I ran inside, I could hear Esperanza call out, "*Hasta mañana, Charlito.*" I didn't answer again.

The minute I pushed the gate open and went inside, I saw Sammie leaning against the screen door of the clubhouse, her arms folded across her chest.

"Have a nice evening?" she said. Her voice was tight and angry.

"Sammie, let me explain . . ."

"Dad already did. I know the whole story. We had a lot of time to talk about it while I *wasn't* out to dinner with you as we had planned. Nice touch, sis."

Ryan came swaggering in from the kitchen, eating ice cream from the carton.

"Somebody's in the doghouse with Sam-I-Am," he said, a few chocolate chips spewing from his mouth. "And I think her initials are C. D. Do you know anyone with those initials, Charles?"

"Can you please ingest your half gallon of ice cream somewhere else, Ryan? Sammie and I need to talk."

"Stay right there, Ryan," Sammie said. "We don't need to talk. I think Charlie's actions tonight said plenty."

"I'm sorry about tonight, Sams," I said. "I was hoping we could go to Barone's tomorrow night."

"I'm busy tomorrow night, Charlie. "

"I know you're not."

"You just don't get it, do you?" Sammie said, her blue eyes glaring at me. "It feels really terrible to be second choice. You chose Lauren and those girls over me. And this isn't the first time, either. So fine. That's the way it is. "

"Score a point for Sammie," Ryan said. "You got a comeback for that, Charles?"

"No, she doesn't," Sammie said. "Because there's really nothing more to say, is there, Charlie? The truth is the truth."

She was right. The truth was that I had missed my friends; that more than anything, I wanted to be back in their company; that I loved the idea of being a Junior Wave; and I had chosen those things over her.

There was a moment of silence, filled only by the slurping sounds of Ryan getting the last goopy remains of Mint Chip from the bottom of the ice-cream carton.

"I'm going to bed," Sammie said.

She turned around and marched inside, leaving me standing there alone, with nothing but my decision to keep me company.

A Nearly Perfect Day

....

Chapter 7

Sammie had already left for school by the time I woke up the next morning. She'd taped a note for me on the shower door.

"I guess you have to do what you have to do," it said. "Good luck with that."

It was a typical Sammie note. She can be really pigheaded about her own ideas. She likes to see things her way. Maybe we all do, I don't know. But as far as I'm concerned, I wasn't sympathetic. I had apologized for standing her up. I had invited her out to another dinner. I had gone to her stupid Truth Tellers, and tried my best to fit in. But it didn't work out. For the first time in weeks, I woke up in a good mood and was looking forward to going to school. You'd think she could be happy for me.

Once I got to school, I couldn't keep myself from hanging around outside Principal Pfeiffer's office. I tried not to be obvious about it, pretending I had developed a deep interest in the policies about respecting school property posted on the bulletin board outside his office. Finally, just before the bell rang, Lauren and Lily came bouncing out into the hall.

"We did it!" Lauren said, linking her arm in mine and guiding me down the hall toward homeroom.

"What did he say?" I asked.

"That he was very familiar with The Waves at Pacific High, and that he thought a Junior Waves at Beachside was a fine idea."

"And guess what, Charlie?" Lily said. "He'd heard about your win at the Sand and Surf tournament over the weekend and was very impressed. Apparently, he has a little son who is just getting started in tennis and thinks you guys are amazing."

"Yay, me!" I said with a giddy laugh. "So when's he going to let us know?"

"He said maybe as early as tomorrow," Lauren answered. "Thursday at the latest. And you know what that means?"

I didn't, but I nodded my head anyway.

"That we could go to the Friday night game as official Junior Waves?" Lily asked.

Lauren didn't answer. She just squealed, and that said it all.

As we walked to homeroom, we talked excitedly

about our ideas for T-shirts. Lily didn't think ours should be exactly the same as the ones The Waves wore, because we wanted to have our own look. But we all agreed that they should definitely be the same color, so when we sat together at the game, we could blend in and look like one big group.

I didn't have a chance to talk with Sammie at school in the morning, but I did run into her at the beginning of lunch. She was standing at her locker with Alicia and Sara Berlin, pulling out a beat-up-looking canvas lunch bag that had seen one too many tuna sandwiches.

"Hi," I said, not too friendly, not too angry, just right in the middle. I wondered if Sammie had told Alicia and Sara about our fight, but I was pretty sure she hadn't because Sara was really friendly and said, "Hey, Charlie. Want to join us for lunch? We're going to Mr. Walsh's room to watch a documentary on how dolphins are almost as intelligent as humans."

"Thanks, Sara, but I can't."

"Charlie has plans with her other group," Sammie said. "I guess we're not good enough for her."

Even Sara and Alicia looked surprised at her tone.

"Ease up there," Alicia said. "This is your sister, you're talking to."

"That's okay," I said to Alicia. "Sammie and I are just having a little disagreement. No big deal. We'll get over it. We always do, don't we, Sams?"

She didn't answer. Fine, that was her choice. I said

good-bye to the others and continued down the hall out to the lunch pavilion. It was a nice breezy day and kids were streaming in, carrying trays of food and cups of yogurt and icy drinks. I glanced over at the spot I knew so well, and there they were—the SF2s. Sean and Jared were on one side of the bench, wedged in between Ben Feldman and the General. Lauren was balancing a tray with three yogurts and climbing over the other bench to sit down. I paused, suddenly feeling unsure if I was going to be welcome. I hoped Lauren would look up and wave me over, but she was busy chatting with Brooke.

"You coming to join us?" said a voice from behind me. I turned around to see Spencer, balancing two cheeseburgers and a large drink on a tray.

"Oh, Spencer. Hi. I mean, hi, Spencer." I heard myself gushing and tried to stop. "I was just wondering if it's okay to be at the table."

"There's only one way to find out," he said, flashing me a hint of dimple.

I followed him to the table, and when I got there, Lauren made a spot for me next to her.

"Sit here, Charlie," she said. "I got you a yogurt. Small low-fat vanilla, no toppings, right? See, I haven't forgotten."

I took a seat. Sean and Jared both put down their subs and stared at me, definitely not in a good way.

"So is everyone okay with this?" Jared said. He didn't even bother to say my name. I was just a "this."

"Yup, we are," Lauren said. "We decided that Charlie is coming back to the group."

"She is? Why?" Jared asked.

"I have my reasons," was all Lauren said. It wasn't exactly a declaration of love for me, but it was good enough. "So you two guys are just going to have to deal with it," Lauren said with authority.

"What if we can't?" Sean answered, trying to stare her down. But Lauren was not going to back down. She just stared at Sean.

"Just grow up," she snapped.

"Easy for you to say," the General said to her, rising to the defense of his two friends. "You're not the one busting your butt varnishing the deck, sweeping sand off the tennis courts, and pulling up weeds like a gardener."

"Why don't we take a vote on whether or not Charlie can stay?" Brooke said. "This is America, and we're a democracy after all."

"Yeah," Jillian jumped in. "Just like they do on *Teens Got Talent*. Last night they voted off that creepy girl who was a contortionist. She could totally dislocate both shoulders and then put them back in the sockets. It was disgusting."

Everyone looked at me like I was going to suddenly stand up and do some kind of freaky body trick. It was so embarrassing. I was beginning to feel sorry that I had sat down at the table at all.

"Whoa, guys," Spencer said, jamming in next to

me on the bench. "Stop talking about Charlie like she's not here. We don't need to vote on anything. Charlie's our friend. Jared and Sean, you messed up and have to take the consequences. I say we move on."

"All in favor raise your hand," Brooke said.

"No, Brooke! You missed the whole point," Spencer said. "We don't have to vote on this. You don't vote on what's the right thing to do. You just do it."

"Listen to you," Ben Feldman said. "The politician's son. When are you running for city council, Ballard?"

Everyone laughed, and suddenly, the tension broke. Jared and Sean went back to eating their sandwiches, Lauren passed me the yogurt, and before I knew it, everyone was talking about their plans for after school.

Lily asked me if I wanted to help shop for stuff to decorate the hats for Bethany's party. Lily's mom was taking her to one of her favorite vintage stores.

Lauren wanted to come along, too. And I was of course in.

As everyone finished lunch, Lauren told us about how impressed the principal was when she said I would be part of the club. As I ate my yogurt, Spencer on one side of me and Lauren on the other, bragging her head off about me, I couldn't believe how dramatically my life had suddenly improved. Everything I wanted was right there at that table. It was almost too good to be true.

After lunch, I went to Ms. Carew's fifth-period

English. When I walked in, she smiled at me like we shared a secret, but never mentioned a word about what had happened at Truth Tellers the day before. Her quote of the day, which she always writes on the blackboard before class, was from a French writer named Pamela Kline.

How I feel about myself is more important than how I look. Feeling confident, being comfortable in your own skin—that's what really makes you beautiful.

I had a feeling Ms. Carew had picked that quote especially for Sara. I glanced over at Sara, and she was writing it down in her black-and-white speckled notebook. Her hair was especially poufy and the curls bobbed up and down as she scribbled. It's weird, I thought, how no one but the Truth Tellers, and me, knew what was hiding under her hair. I was among the few people in the whole world who understood why that quote meant so much to her. I wasn't sure I wanted that information, but like it or not, I had it.

As soon as school let out, Lily's mom was waiting for us in a beautiful navy-blue convertible.

"You guys want the top down?" she asked as we climbed in.

"Duh," Lily said.

Her mom laughed, pushed a button, and within seconds, the top lifted off, folded up, and tucked itself into the trunk. As we drove off, I saw Sammie walking with Alicia and Sara. I waved, but only Alicia waved back. Sammie pretended not to see me.

But I didn't give Sammie a second thought as we cruised down Pacific Coast Highway, our hair blowing in our faces and the radio blaring. The only thing that kept going through my head was: *Could this day get any better?*

Believe it or not, it did.

Lily's mom, who designs swimsuits—or as she calls it, swimwear—took us to *Yesterday's Treasures*, her favorite vintage store in Venice, which is this funky area a couple miles down the beach from the club. The shelves were piled up to the ceiling with old clothes and flower vases and swatches of fabric and jewelry and buttons and weird sunglasses and anything else you could think of.

"This place is a treasure trove," she said. "Dig in, girls, and see what you can find."

Lily instructed us to look for old hats and interesting things she could use to decorate them with. I found a white sea captain's hat buried under a pile of moldy magazines, and a crazy-looking orange straw hat with a purple brim. I even pulled out a construction worker's bright-yellow hard hat. Lauren unearthed a glamorous little black velvet hat that had a lace veil in the front and a well-used Detroit Tigers baseball cap. Mrs. March had the find of the day, though—an old-school Girl Scout beanie with a little green tassel on the top. She thought that it might be from the 1970s. Lily spent most of her time collecting buttons and scarves and glittery jewelry that would make each hat original and fun.

After an hour, we had collected a big pile of stuff. Mrs. March bargained with Claude, the shop owner, who she seemed to know pretty well. They settled on a price of twenty-five dollars for everything.

"That was the most fun thing ever," I said as we walked out carrying everything in brown grocery bags.

"I can't wait to show all our treasures to Bethany," Lily said. "She's going to be so excited."

"Let's go show her now," Lauren suggested. "She texted earlier that she was at the club."

I didn't want everyone going back there in case we'd run into Sammie. She was in such a bad mood, there's no telling what she'd say to them. But I couldn't think of a reason to say no, so we got in the car and Lily's mom dropped us off at the club. I was so relieved when we went inside and Sammie was nowhere in sight. Bethany was sitting at a table outside, drinking a bottle of water.

"How'd the shopping go?" she asked.

"Wait until I show you all the cool stuff we got," Lily said to her. "We have enough for seven or eight hats, and I've already designed some others."

"This is so amazing," Bethany said. "Let's lay everything out."

The two outside tables were reserved for the ladies bridge club, so we went inside the clubhouse. GoGo was in the kitchen, experimenting with kebab marinades for Bethany's party. She thought kebabs would go better with mini quiches than chicken drumettes. My dad was having a meeting in the living room with two men about possibly adding a locker room and resurfacing the tennis courts. They had plans and blueprints spread out all over the coffee table. No space was available.

"No problemo," Lauren said to me. "Let's just go to your room and lay everything out on your bed."

Before I could say anything, she headed toward the bedroom I share with Sammie. Our bedroom door was closed with a sign tacked up on it. It was in big, red letters, in Sammie's handwriting.

PRIVATE! it said. DO NOT EVEN THINK ABOUT COMING IN HERE.

Lauren looked at it and laughed, then with her usual swagger, pushed the door open.

"You can't go in there!" I shouted to her.

But it was too late.

Ears and Hats

....

Chapter 8

"Hey! Didn't you see the sign?" Sammie yelled. She practically threw her body in front of Lauren to stop her from entering our room. Lauren tried to peek around Sammie, to get a glimpse of what was going on.

"What's the big secret, anyway?" she asked.

By that time, I had caught up with her. I quickly glanced into our room. I could see Sara and Alicia standing by the far wall. Sammie was doing her best to block them from our view.

"Get her out of here," Sammie warned me. "I'm not kidding, Charlie. Now!"

"Come on," I said, taking Lauren's arm. "Let's go."

"It's your room, too," she grumbled. "Sammie has no right to keep you out of it."

Sammie stepped into the hall and closed the bedroom door behind her.

"I think you should mind your own business, Lauren. And that goes for her, too," she snapped, pointing her finger at someone behind me.

I turned around to see Bethany.

"Sammie? Tell me what's going on," I said.

"Alicia and Sara and I are busy. That's all you need to know. If you guys come in, I'll never forgive you."

"Wow, that's intense," Bethany said.

"Let's just go back into the kitchen," I suggested, trying to lighten up the situation. "I'll ask my grandmother if we can use the counter."

"But I don't want to get kebab juice on my hats," Bethany said.

"We'll be really careful," I promised. I steered Lauren and Bethany away from the door. Just before I left, I turned to Sammie and said, "Don't worry. We're going now."

"Good," she said. "And don't come back."

Then she opened the door and disappeared inside.

GoGo was really nice and cleared off the whole counter for us. She put the bowls with different kebab marinades on top of the stove instead. "We've got curry, herb and garlic, and pineapple-soy," she said. "I think your friends will have lots of tasty choices, Bethany."

"Do I get to do a tasting before the party?" Bethany asked. GoGo seemed quite surprised at that. "When my parents had their twenty-fifth anniversary party," Bethany went on, "they had lots of tastings until they felt the chef finally got the menu right."

"Well, dear," GoGo began. I knew what was coming. Whenever GoGo calls someone dear, it means she's annoyed. "When you've been married twenty-five years, perhaps you'll have lots of tastings, too. But you're only sixteen, and I think you're going to have to trust the chef on this one."

GoGo wiped off the counter with a damp cloth to make sure it was clean.

"You girls can put your things here," she said. "I'm going down to the beach to watch the sunset."

As soon as GoGo left, Lily opened up the bags and started to put the hats on the counter. I wasn't paying much attention, though. I kept glancing toward my bedroom. I really wanted to know what was going on in there. Lauren noticed and smiled a mischievous smile.

"Me too," she said, even though I hadn't said anything.

"Me too what?"

"Let's just say it. We're both dying to know what's happening. It's your room, too. You have a right to know. Let's go listen at the door and see if we can hear anything."

"Lauren! That's so not nice," Bethany said. "Let's do it."

"No, you guys," I pleaded. "Please don't."

"I bet they snuck a boy in there," Bethany giggled. "Who do you think it is?"

"There's no boy in there," I told her. "I promise you that."

"Well, what else could be so secret that if you found out, Sammie would never forgive you?" Lauren asked.

Bethany slipped off her shoes.

"Take your shoes off, too, Lauren, so we can tiptoe over there without a sound."

This was getting out of hand.

"Okay," I said. "I tell you what. I'll go see if they'll let me in. If it's anything interesting, I'll come back and tell you. If it isn't, we can just forget it and work on the hats."

"You promise?" Lauren said.

I nodded and hurried off across our living room and down the tiny hall to our bedroom before they could change their minds.

"Sammie?" I whispered, knocking at the door again. "Let me in."

"Who's with you?"

"No one. I swear."

I heard her whispering with Alicia and Sara, then a rushing around of footsteps. After a few seconds, Sammie cracked open the door and stuck her head out.

"What do you want?"

"Just let me in." I pushed by her and went inside,

expecting to be really surprised by something I saw. I didn't think it would be a boy, but knowing Sammie, it could have been a stray dog. We had seen a lost-looking German Shepherd on the beach the other morning, and Sammie wanted to take him home. Our dad said no, even after she begged him.

I looked around our room. No dog. No boys. No nothing. Just Alicia and Sara standing around with secretive looks on their faces.

"What's going on in here?" I asked.

"Nothing," they all said at once. They were obviously hiding something.

I saw Sammie reach behind her back and tuck something into the waistband of her jeans.

"What's in your jeans, then?"

"Just a brush. No big deal."

I glanced at Sammie's bed and noticed that it was draped with four or five colorful scarves that belonged to our mom. One of them was clearly GoGo's, because it had pink flamingos all over it. I saw two or three of my headbands lying on the pillow next to a floppy white tennis hat that I wear on really sunny days. Our mom's hand mirror, the one that is regular on one side and magnifying on the other, was sitting on the pillow, too. And next to it was Sammie's cell phone.

"Why are you using my hair stuff?" I asked. "And GoGo's scarves?

No one answered.

"Come on, you guys," I said. "This is my room, too,

and I need to know what's going on in here."

"We're just doing something for Sara," Alicia said. "A project."

"For school?" I asked.

"Kind of," Sammie said. "You might say that."

"Oh, so now we're playing twenty questions?" I was getting annoyed. "It really hurts my feelings that you don't trust me enough to tell me the truth."

That got their attention. You mention the Truth (with a capital T) around these girls and the whole world stops.

"It's up to Sara whether or not to tell you," Alicia said. "It's her decision."

"I guess it's okay if we tell her," Sara answered. "We're trying to come up with some different looks for me so I don't always have to wear my hair down."

"To make her less sensitive about that issue she spoke of yesterday," Alicia said.

"Her ears?"

"Of course her ears," Sammie barked. "I can't believe you even have to ask that."

"I'm trying on all kinds of scarves and headbands and hats to see what looks best," Sara said. "I haven't been able to change my hairstyle since I started middle school because of, you know, the Dumbo thing."

The minute she said that, big tears formed in her eyes. "And your sister and Alicia are being so sweet to me. They're even taking before and after pictures."

I saw Sammie reach out and pick up her phone, protectively.

"Don't worry, I'm not going to peek," I said, "unless you want to show me."

"Maybe we could show Charlie the look I think is the cutest—the one where we wrapped your Grandma's scarf around her head, pirate-style," Alicia said. "Just to get another opinion. What do you think, Sara?"

"Okay, you can show her."

Sammie held out her phone and I took it. The first thing that came up on the screen was a picture of Sara with her usual poufy hair. The next shot was Sara with her hair pulled on top of her head so you could see the full ear problem. I hadn't really looked at her ears closely during Truth Tellers. It's not exactly the kind of thing you feel comfortable staring at. But now, I could see why they bothered her so much. The picture reminded me of the toy Mr. Potato Head. Sammie and I used to play with the plastic potato when we were younger. He came with these big pink plastic ears that stuck straight out from his head.

I don't mean to sound rude. Sara's ears weren't as bad as Mr. Potato Head's. But they were definitely in the same category, if you know what I mean.

The third picture showed Sara's hair all covered up with GoGo's flamingo scarf. It was wrapped around her head tightly and tied in a fancy knot at the back. The scarf held her ears back so only the very tips showed, and Sammie had put some gold hoops on them.

"You look great here," I said to Sara, and I meant it.

"You don't think I look too much like Captain Hook?" she asked.

"Not unless you have a crocodile chasing after you."

"I think Sara would appreciate it if you wouldn't crack jokes at a time like this," Sammie complained. As far as she was concerned, I couldn't do anything right.

Pardon me for breathing.

Just then, someone knocked at the door. Sammie lunged at me and grabbed the phone, turning off the screen in one swift motion.

"Charlie," Lily called through the door. "Come on. We're all ready."

"It's just Lily," I told them. "Can I show the pictures to her? She's such a creative clothes designer, and she's making a ton of hats for Bethany's party. I'll bet she'd have some great suggestions for you."

"Don't you dare," Sammie said. "This is something we talked about in Truth Tellers. And what we say in Truth Tellers stays in Truth Tellers. That's our motto."

"Okay, okay. I get it. I was just trying to help."

There was another knock at the door and this time, I heard Lauren talking.

"You're holding everything up, Charlie. Come on."

"And never breathe a word of this to her," Sammie

said. "She can't be trusted. You and I both know that, but you just won't admit it."

There it was again. Sammie was never going to let this go. She obviously could not forgive and forget. One day, we'll probably be forty years old and she'll still be telling me about how bad a friend Lauren Wadsworth was to me.

I put my hand on the doorknob and turned it.

"Careful not to let her see in when you're going out," Sammie warned.

I slid out of the door sideways and closed it behind me. Lily had already gone back into the kitchen, but Lauren and Bethany were standing on their tiptoes trying to see inside. "Well? What was it? Was there a guy in there? I bet it was that Devon kid. He's kind of hot for a weirdo," Lauren said.

"What are they hiding?" Bethany asked. "Are they in trouble? Did they steal something? Was it jewelry?"

"Sorry, I can't tell you," I answered as we walked back to the kitchen. "I'm pledged to secrecy. But it's none of those things, and it's not that interesting, anyhow."

"You're really not going to tell us?" Lauren was amazed.

"Uh, that's what secrecy means, brainiac," Lily said, laughing. "Now come on, Lauren, refocus. We've got creative work to do here."

Lily held up each of our purchases and described how she was planning to use it. For instance, she was going to make pink velvet bows and put them all over the hard hat to show that girls could be construction workers, too. Then she held up this old rhinestone pin that was shaped like a cookie. She put it on the front of the Girl Scout beanie.

"I love that one," Bethany said, taking out her phone and snapping a picture of it. "I'm going to post it on Instagram."

"Don't show it to everyone before the party," Lily protested. "It'll ruin the surprise."

"I'll just do this one," Bethany said.

By then, GoGo had returned from the beach and joined us.

"What's Instagram?" she asked. I was surprised she hadn't heard about it, because even though she's a grandma, she's pretty up on current things.

"It's a photo-sharing site," I explained. "People take pictures and post them so everyone can see and comment on them."

"Oh my," GoGo said. "Isn't anything private anymore? Does the world have to see everything we're all doing every minute?"

"It's really fun," Bethany said. "I post all the time."

"Do you and Sammie do this Insta . . . whatever you call it?" GoGo asked me.

"We can't yet. You have to have a smartphone to have Instagram. And besides, Mom and Dad would probably never let us get it."

Bethany smirked at me and then showed GoGo the picture she had posted of the Girl Scout hat with the cookie. There were already three comments. A girl name Jenna had said, "One year, I ate all the Thin Mints before I even sold a box." Someone named Lizzy had written, "Dork City." And Bethany's boyfriend had posted, "See you later, cookie."

"See how much fun it is?" Bethany said. "You get instant feedback."

"I think what we're doing right here in real life is much more fun," GoGo said. "Lily, show us what else you've created."

Lily went on demonstrating her ideas. When GoGo saw the bright-orange straw hat I had picked out, she clapped her hands with pleasure.

"Love the color," she exclaimed. "I have an old scarf with pink flamingos that would look stunning as a band on that hat. Wait right here and I'll get it."

I didn't say a word, just watched as GoGo went to her room and came back empty-handed.

"That's a mystery," she said. "I could have sworn I saw it in my closet this morning."

"Maybe it got up and walked into Sammie's room," Lauren said, making her voice sound all mysterious and creepy like a zombie. "There seem to be a lot of secrets going on in there."

Everybody laughed. I laughed, too, a little too loud, the way you do when you're trying to cover something up—like the fact that the flamingo scarf really was in our room.

"I can't wait to see everyone wearing these hats Saturday night," Bethany said. "And then when we all take them off and throw them in my honor—it's going to be awesome. It's too bad you guys won't be there to see it."

"We could be if you'd invite us," Lauren hinted.

"I don't mean to insult you, but this is a high-school party. You guys wouldn't fit in. You don't even know my friends."

"But if our application for Junior Waves gets approved, we'll be at the football game Friday night, and we could sit together with you guys and meet everyone," Lauren argued.

"We wouldn't have to stay for the whole party," Lily chimed in. "We could leave right after the hat throwing."

"I could bring my brother, Ryan, and he's in the eighth grade," I added. It wasn't the strongest argument, but it was the best I had at the moment.

Bethany hesitated.

"I'll be sure to make enough kebabs for everyone," GoGo said, emphasizing the word *everyone*. She's so great. One of the things she always says is, "Why exclude when you can include?" And there she was, taking our side in this.

"Let's wait and see what your principal says about the club," Bethany answered. "But I'm not making any promises."

When it was time to leave, I walked out to the parking lot with Lauren.

"This was such a fun day," I said to her.

"Tomorrow will be even better," she said, "if we get the okay to go ahead with Junior Waves. And wait until you hear what I have planned for us. It's epic."

"What is it?" I asked.

"Initiation," she whispered. "Tests of loyalty. Mysterious ceremonies. Weird dangerous stuff."

"Like what?"

"First tell me what was going on in your room with Sammie and those girls," she bargained.

"I can't."

"Oh, come on," she begged. "I dare you. I double dare you."

"I really can't say, Lauren."

"Well, then I can't say what my epic plan is. Maybe you'll find out, maybe you won't."

"Lauren, that's not fair!"

"I know," she said, and I heard her laughing all the way to the car.

It's Official

....

Chapter 9

"We got it!" Lauren screamed. "Look, read this!"

It was the next day, and I was sitting at the lunch table with the SF2s.

"Read what it says, Lauren," Brooke said. "Don't skip one word."

Everyone was focused on Lauren, who was standing at the head of the table. She cleared her throat.

"From the Office of Principal Peter S. Pfeiffer," she began dramatically. "I have granted permission for the formation of a new school club called the Junior Waves. The charter members are Lauren Wadsworth, Brooke Addison, Jillian Kendall—"

"That's me," Jillian squealed.

"I think we all know that, Jilly," Ben Feldman said.

"—Lily March, and Charlie Diamond. Pretty amazing, huh, guys?"

"Is that all it says?" Jared asked. "There's a ton more written on that paper. I can see it from here."

"Honestly, Jared, what I just read is the only important part. It goes on with all this stuff about how we have to maintain our grade point average and participate in school-sponsored community service. Junk like that."

"Thank goodness we have Charlie for all that," Jillian said.

I know what Sammie would have said about her comment, that they were just using me to get the club approved. But I put that out of my mind and instead tried to feel proud that I was doing my share to help us all become Junior Waves.

"Anything else?" Lily asked.

"Nothing much," Lauren said. "There's this whole paragraph that goes on and on about how we can't be exclusive or discriminate against anyone, blah, blah, blah."

"Whoa, there," Brooke said, holding up her hand. "Does that mean we have to let anyone who wants to join?"

"What's wrong with that?" Spencer said.

"But I thought this was *our* club."

"It will be our club," Lauren said. "We'll be the founders and the officers and run it. We'll be the Core Four, just like always. Jilly, Brooks, Lilykins, and me."

Wait a minute. Where was I in that list? I was missing, that's where I was. I sat there at the table, feeling like someone had punched me in the stomach, but I was too intimidated to say anything.

"Wait, what about Charlie?" Lily said. "She's the whole reason we got permission to form the club in the first place."

"Oh, wow, did I leave Charlie out?" Lauren said. I couldn't tell if she was faking it. "I'm sorry."

"That's okay," I said, although I wasn't sure I really meant it.

"Then it's official," Lauren went on, with a wave in my direction. She pretended to pound an imaginary gavel on the table. "I'm announcing that the first meeting of the Junior Waves is today after school at my house. Is everybody in?"

"I can't do it," Lily said. "I've got to go home to work on the hats. I've finished fifteen, but I'm still only halfway done."

"But we need you, Lily." Lauren seemed annoyed with her. "Who's going to design our T-shirts? We've got to get them printed before Friday if we're going to wear them to the game."

"Maybe we just won't wear them to this week's game," I suggested. "We can always wait until the next game."

"That's a terrible idea, Charlie," Lauren snapped. "This is the most important week to wear them. We have to make a good impression on Bethany's friends and the high-school kids. Unless you guys just don't want to get invited to her party."

"Oh, we do," Brooke and Jillian said in unison.

"So then we need our T-shirts right away," Lauren declared. "That's all there is to it."

"Okay, maybe I can get my mom to help," Lily said. "Actually, she's the one who designed the T-shirts and bags for The Waves. She's at home today doing a photo shoot for her new line of cover-ups. I'll text her. We could meet at my house later to see what she's done."

Lauren looked unhappy with this plan.

"The first meeting should really be held at the president's house," she said.

"So now Lauren's the president?" Spencer said, shaking his head at the rest of us. "I don't remember you guys having an election."

"Well, I just assumed that since it was all my idea in the first place, I'd be the president," Lauren answered.

"I don't think that's the way elections work." Spencer looked annoyed. "This may come as a total shock, but you're not the boss of everyone, Lauren."

The whole group got real quiet. It was highly unusual for anyone in the SF2s to question Lauren's authority, and we were all waiting to see what she'd do. She didn't like it one bit, I can tell you that.

"Just because your father's on city council, it doesn't mean you know everything about elections and politics and how to run things, Spencer," she snapped, putting her hands on her hips. "I haven't noticed you forming a club, so what do you know about clubs, anyway?"

"Spencer is on three sports teams," I heard myself saying. "He's also in the Heal the Bay Club and the Multicultural Club. I think he knows a thing or two about participation."

I surprised myself at my firm tone of voice and ability to stand up to Lauren in front of everyone. I certainly hadn't planned to do it, but when she attacked Spencer, the words just fell out of my mouth. What was an even bigger surprise was that Lauren gave in.

"Okay, fine," she said. "I'm in too good a mood to argue. If it's so important to everyone, we'll meet at Lily's house. Four o'clock. Don't be late, we have a lot to do."

I had to go to my locker before fifth period, so I got up to leave before the lunch bell rang. Spencer got up, too, and walked with me across the lawn. It was a gorgeous day, and I couldn't help but notice the way the sun was shining on Spencer's blond hair. His hair is dark blond and curly, so the sunlight just caught the ends and for some reason, it reminded me of a plate of crispy curly fries.

I kind of laughed to myself.

"What's so funny?" he asked.

"I was just thinking that your hair looks like curly fries," I confessed.

"And . . . that's a good thing or a bad thing?"

"Oh good. Very good. I love curly fries."

I winced right after I said that. Had I just told Spencer Ballard that I loved him? I hope I hadn't, even though I think I might actually love him. Certainly big-time like.

"Thanks for sticking up for me back there," he said. "Lauren can bite like a shark when she feels like it."

"She's got a lot of natural leadership skills," I said.

He laughed out loud.

"I like Lauren," he said. "We've been friends forever. But let's face it, she can definitely be mean when she wants to be."

I didn't say anything. Lauren and I were at the beginning of rebuilding our friendship, and I didn't want to be disloyal to her in any way.

"So it seems you're pretty familiar with my activities," Spencer said. "You almost know more about what I do than me."

I was so embarrassed, I wanted to transform into a worm, drop into the grass, and slither away. It never occurred to me when I was speaking up that I was also revealing my interest in Spencer. He probably thought I was some kind of stalker.

"I just . . . um . . . have this photographic memory for stuff like that," I said. "Details plant themselves in my brain and stay there."

Shut up, Charlie. This isn't helping. He doesn't care about your memory. You sound like you're a science experiment.

Thank goodness we had reached my locker. I wanted to put my face inside it and slam the door.

"Well, I have to go change for PE," he said. "So I'll see you around."

"Bye," I answered, unable to look him in the face.

He headed down the hall, and I focused intently on my locker combination, twirling that little knob around like it was a spinning top.

"Oh by the way, Charlie," he said, turning to me just before he rounded the corner. "I know all your activities, too."

He shot me a full dimple smile, and then he walked away.

A Secret Pact

"I think it's that house over there," I said to my dad as he drove a mile an hour down Sea Breeze Lane looking for Lily's house. "Lily said it looks like a log cabin only without the logs."

"That makes zero sense," Sammie piped up from the backseat. "A log cabin without logs is not a log cabin and therefore couldn't possibly look like one."

"Fine, Sammie," I said. "You win. I'm just repeating what Lily said."

I didn't want to argue with her. We had just finished a tennis practice where we actually spoke to each other, and had even managed to give each other a few compliments like "nice shot" or "good serve." It wasn't exactly kisses and hugs, but it was slightly better than the icy stares she had been giving me.

I had never been to Lily's house before. She doesn't usually invite people over after school, since both her parents work at home and we'd be in the way. Her dad is a record producer and her mom is a fashion designer. They spend a lot of time in the studio they built in the backyard.

"I don't see a house that looks like a log cabin, with or without logs," my dad said. "All I see are ten-foot-high hedges."

"The house is probably behind one of them," I said. "You can just drop me off, Dad. I'll find it."

"No way, Jose."

He pulled the car to a stop in the middle of the road and started fiddling with his navigation system, trying to plug in Lily's address.

"Dad, I'm already late," I groaned. "I don't have time for this."

Although the newly formed Junior Waves club had agreed to meet at four o'clock precisely, my dad had insisted I come home after school to practice with Sammie for an hour. When I complained, he reminded me that I had agreed to put school and tennis first before Junior Waves. Then after tennis, we had to wait another ten minutes for Sammie to find her stupid Spanish book so that after he dropped me off, he could drop her off at Alicia's house to study. I knew Sara would be there, too, because Sammie asked if she could borrow some more of my headbands and my gray-and-white striped beanie.

Lily's house was not at all what we were expecting. We had been looking for something low and small and Abe Lincoln-like. But her house, which was behind tall hedges at the end of the cul-de-sac, was a huge two-story modern house that was nestled into the hillside and seemed to rise out of the trees. I guess you could say it was made of logs. Under its A-shaped roof were two stories of floor to ceiling windows, and a chimney made of giant smooth rocks. It was one of the most beautiful houses I'd ever seen.

"That's quite a log cabin," my dad said, letting out an admiring whistle. "Maybe one day, if you girls win Wimbledon, you can buy yourselves a place like that."

I could tell that looking at Lily's house made my dad sad. Our old house in Culver City was never grand like this one, but it did have four bedrooms, a big family room, and even a swimming pool in the backyard. When he lost his job and my mom left for school, we had to sell it and move to our cramped quarters at the club.

"You got it, Dad," Sammie said, giving him a pat on the shoulder. "In fact, we'll buy two of them."

"Yeah, one for us and one for you and Mom," I agreed.

"What about Ryan?"

"Nope. He has to live in another city until he becomes way less annoying," Sammie said with a chuckle.

"Maybe even another continent," I added. Then

we both burst out laughing.

"That's better," my dad said. "That's the way I like to see my girls."

I climbed out of the car and Sammie crawled over into the front seat.

"I'll be back here at six thirty," my dad hollered out the window. "And Charlie, don't call and ask if you can stay later, because the answer will be no. You've got homework to do."

As they drove away, I walked up the driveway and rang the doorbell. The front door was made of copper, with trees and leaves and birds etched on the front. The bell was also encased in copper, as if it was the center of a blooming copper rose. I was looking at the door so intently that I jumped when it opened and a person I'd never seen before was standing there. She was a young African American woman, maybe twenty years old, wearing a pair of jeans and a sweatshirt that said Stanford University.

"Uh, is this Lily March's house?" I asked.

"Yes. I'm Neela, her sister."

"Oh. I didn't know she had a sister." That sounded rude, so I quickly added, "No offense or anything, I'm sure she told me and I just forgot."

Neela laughed.

"I'm her half-sister. Same dad, different mom. Most of the time, I'm away at college so she probably doesn't talk about me a lot."

"I'm kind of new to the group," I told her. "So I'm

just getting to know everyone's family."

"You must be Charlie," she said. "The girls told me a little about you."

"I hope it was all good."

Okay, I admit it. I was kind of searching for a compliment, hoping she'd say something like, *"They all just love you and they can't stop talking about how cool you are."* But she didn't say that. In fact, she didn't say anything, just stepped back and opened the door for me.

"Come on in. Lily and the others are out back in our parent's studio. I'll show you where it is."

The inside of the house was even more beautiful than the outside. There wasn't what you'd call a regular living room or family room or dining room or anything. It was just one great big room, with giant pillowy furniture all around. The stark white walls were hung with brightly colored woven rugs. There was a huge stone fireplace in the center of the room and a curving stone staircase that led up to the second-floor loft at the back. All along the stairway hung painted masks of varying shapes and sizes. A few had horns and looked like animals, and others looked like human faces. Some were friendly looking; others were freakishly scary.

"Who are those guys?" I asked Neela as we passed by.

"Those are tribal masks," she said. "I brought them back from Africa for my dad."

"Do you live there?"

"No, but I did a year of college there. I'm majoring in cultural anthropology, which is a fancy way to say I'm studying groups of people."

"You have to go to Africa for that? Can't you just do it in the mall?"

Neela laughed.

"I study people from different cultures and ways of life. The tribes who made these masks use them in their rituals and ceremonies, which is very foreign to us."

"We learned about Native American rituals in social studies," I said. "They did some pretty cool stuff, like dances to make it rain and protect them from evil spirits. They were very spiritual."

Neela stopped and turned to me. "I like you, Charlie. You're smart," she said. "Different from the other girls."

"Lily's smart, too."

"Yes, she is. And if I can count correctly, that makes two of you."

I followed Neela through the stainless steel kitchen and out into the backyard. We crossed a stone bridge that led to another wooden building. It was like a mini version of the house. When Neela opened the door and led me inside, I was so blown away my jaw actually dropped. All along the wall were framed Gold Records, the kind that you win for selling a million albums. There must have been twenty-five or thirty of them.

"Our dad's had a pretty nice run of luck," she smiled.

The girls were sitting in a circle on the floor. Lily's hat supplies were laid out in front of them. It looked like Lily had finished another five or six, including a cowboy hat with peacock and eagle feathers and a red velvet turban with fake gold coins draped across the front.

"Finally, you're here," Lauren said to me. "We've been waiting for you for half an hour."

"Sorry I'm late. I had to finish tennis practice before my dad would let me come over."

"No worries," Lily said. "It gave me time to finish these hats while we were waiting."

"I get to decide if it's fine or not," Lauren stood up and took control of the conversation. "While we were waiting for you, we officially elected me president."

"You have my vote, too," I said. "Or at least, you would've if I had been here."

"That's what I thought," Lauren said. "So I voted in your place and we called it unanimous."

"Democracy in action." Neela chuckled.

Neela went over to a desk near the window, sat down, and turned on the computer.

"Uh, Neela. No offense, but this is a private meeting," Lauren said. "So . . . could you do that somewhere else?"

"No offense back at you," Neela said, "but when I'm home, I sleep in the studio, so technically you guys are in my space."

Lauren glanced at Lily, but Lily just shrugged. "Neela's cool," she said. "Let's just go on with our meeting."

"Okay." Lauren sighed. "I guess we have no choice. Let's begin with the plans for the T-shirts."

"My mom already did a preliminary design," Lily said. "I waited to show everyone until Charlie got here."

"Which I said was fine," Lauren added. "So we're ready to look at it now. But before we do, we all have to take a pledge of secrecy. No one but us can know what the T-shirts look like until we arrive at the game on Friday. Raise your right hand and repeat after me."

We did as we were told. This was fun. Everyone loves a secret pact. And Jillian said it was just like the pledge contestants make on *Teen Survivor*.

"As a member of the Junior Waves," we repeated after Lauren, "I do solemnly swear not to reveal to anyone what we are about to see."

After the oath, Lily went to her mom's drafting table and returned with a large sheet of drawing paper that was covered with a sheet of taped-on tracing paper. She sat down, but just before she flipped the tracing paper up, Lauren stopped her.

"Wait," she said. "Don't show the design yet. There's someone here who has not taken the oath." She glanced over at Neela, who was typing something on the computer.

Neela looked up.

"Are you talking to me?"

Lauren nodded. Neela just laughed.

"I'm afraid I'm going to have to insist that you take our sacred oath," Lauren said.

Neela laughed again.

"Listen, girlfriend, I've studied tribal oaths on three continents," she said. "And I have never seen one that involves a T-shirt. So if you girls want to do it, fine, but don't involve me."

Without waiting for Lauren's approval, Lily just went ahead and lifted the tracing paper to reveal the design. It was set against a turquoise background, just like the Waves shirts and bags were. But the design itself was totally different, done in a fluorescent orange. Taking up the whole front of the shirt was a drawing of a beautiful, Chinese-looking folding fan, half-moon shaped. Flowing across its folds was a long foamy wave that was about to break. Under the drawing, orange letters said, "The Junior Waves—We're Fans!"

It was perfect. Beautiful, different, clever, and so cool. I could hardly stop myself from popping to my feet and jumping up and down like a two year old.

"I don't get it," Jillian said, staring at the design. "What does a fan have to do with waves?"

"Don't you see, Jilly?" I said. "*Fan* and *fan*."

Jillian looked even more confused.

"Let *me* explain," Lauren said. "It's part of my job as president."

Turning to Jillian, Lauren got all serious like the real president does when he's about to give a speech. "The fan on our T-shirt has two meanings," she explained. "When you first look at it, it seems like it's just a fan. But when you think about it, it says something else, too—that the Junior Waves are *fans*. Like we're *fans* of the sports teams. *Fan* and *fan*."

"Ooohhh," Jillian said. "Now I get it."

"Just so everyone knows, as your president, I'm always here to explain things." Lauren seemed very pleased with herself.

"So now that we're all clear on the concept, what do we think?" Lily asked. "Do we like it?"

"It's perfect," I said. "Your mom's a genius. And I, for one, will be proud to wear it to the game Friday night."

"Oh, I'm so glad you love it, Charlie," Lily said. "I think it will look great with jeans."

"I was just about to say that," Lauren said. "My idea is that we need to all go out and buy orange shoes to match the orange on the shirt."

That made me worried. I'm not rich like everyone else, and I sure couldn't just go out and buy shoes whenever I wanted. But then I remembered that I had a pair of never-worn, bright-orange Nike running shoes that Sammie and I were given after we won a Nike Invitational Tournament. They'd look really cute with the shirt.

Phew, that was close.

"And now for the best part," Lauren said. "Gather around because I have something really special to announce."

This was it! This was the epic plan she had talked about in the parking lot. Lauren lowered her voice to almost a whisper and waited until she had everyone's attention.

"Let us never forget that we are the core of this group. We are the heart. We will be true to each other, no matter what. Do we agree on this?"

"Yes," we all whispered at once.

"Then I, as your president, am asking each girl here to take part in a day of initiation tomorrow. I have written down what each of you is to do during the day. You must do everything on the list, exactly as I have written it. And if you do, then I will allow you to take part in tomorrow night's initiation ceremony."

"What ceremony?" Brooke asked.

"The Junior Waves swearing in," Lauren said. "The ceremony where we all officially bond as Wave sisters, for ever and ever."

"This is so exciting," Brooke said. "What's going to happen at the ceremony?"

Neela got up from the desk and walked over to us.

"I think I can help you with this," she said. "I have a lot of experience with initiation ceremonies."

"Way cool," Jillian said. "Are you in a sorority? My mom was a Tri Delt. She said when she got initiated, she had to sit on a whole bunch of balloons filled with shaving cream."

"No, I'm not in a sorority," Neela said. "And that's certainly not the type of initiation I'm talking about. What I study is how people celebrate important moments in their life cycles. Like the birth of children and weddings and funerals."

"Funerals?" Brooke said. "*Eeuuwww,* we're not going to die, are we?"

"I think Neela was just using it as an example," I said, "of the kinds of events people create ceremonies and rituals for."

"Can we hold hands and sing a song?" Brooke asked.

"Actually, those are both very common things that people do in these kinds of ceremonies," Neela said. "They share food and music to create a sense of community. Sometimes they wear costumes or special clothes, like masks or headdresses or jewelry."

"Now you're talking my language," Jillian said. "Lauren, can we wear lots of jewelry at our ceremony?"

"The most important thing that happens in all initiation ceremonies is the sharing of trust," Neela said. "When a community forms and takes new members, people have to prove their loyalty to each other."

"That is exactly what I've been planning for tomorrow," Lauren beamed. "An all-day initiation. You will start by doing everything on the list I've made for you. Remember, as a test of your loyalty, you must do *everything* I ask of you. And you cannot tell anyone that what you are doing is part of our secret initiation. Understood?"

We all nodded. Then Lauren reached into her purse and pulled out four sealed envelopes.

"Inside these envelopes are your initiation assignments," she said. "Each of you will do different things, but the important thing is that you will only be judged loyal enough to come to the initiation ceremony if you complete the list."

"How come you don't have to do any initiation assignments?" Jillian asked.

"I already did mine," Lauren said. "Bethany initiated me. Charlie saw, didn't you, Charlie? I had to walk and cluck like a chicken for an entire afternoon."

"I hope we don't have to do anything embarrassing like that," Brooke said.

"You'll find out when you go home tonight and open your envelopes." Lauren stood up and handed each of us our sealed envelope. "Everyone onboard?"

We nodded.

"Good. Tomorrow is Initiation Day. If everyone does well, we'll meet at sundown on the beach for the final ceremony."

"That's appropriate," Neela said. "Many native ceremonies are held at sundown. It's a very spiritual time of day."

"I know that," Lauren said. "And I think I can take

it from here, Neela."

We ended with forming a circle and holding hands. Oddly enough, this reminded me of the Acceptance Circle they do at a Truth Tellers meeting, but without the humming, of course.

"Until tomorrow then, Junior Waves forever," Lauren said. "And don't breathe a word to anyone."

This was feeling very real. And very mysterious. And incredibly exciting.

I couldn't wait to get home and see what was inside my envelope.

The List

....

Chapter 11

"Charlie!" Ryan yelled, pounding on the bathroom door. "You stay in there any longer and we're going to charge you rent!"

"I'll be out in a few minutes," I hollered back. "I've got to finish drying my hair."

I wasn't drying my hair at all. I hadn't even washed it. But when you live with your whole family in three tiny rooms in a caretaker's cottage, the only place you can go for a little privacy is the bathroom. The other girls in the SF2s were probably opening their envelopes lying on their beds in their own rooms. But me, I had to lock myself in the bathroom and pretend to be drying my hair just to be able to open my envelope and read my initiation assignment list in private.

I read the five items at least twenty times. At the top, in bright pink marker, Lauren had written CHARLIE'S LIST. Under it, she had printed the words: *For Your Eyes Only. Memorize this list, and then destroy it.* After that, came the list.

INITIATION ASSIGNMENTS
1. *Wear one flip-flop and one shoe all day at school.*
2. *Refuse to turn in your Spanish homework.*
3. *Bring me something from Principal Pfeiffer's desk.*
4. *Steal a cookie from Starbucks after school.*

As I poured over the list, I could feel my hands starting to sweat. My armpits, too. This list definitely made me nervous. As bad as clucking like a chicken was, almost everything on this list was a whole lot worse. And wouldn't not turning in my homework jeopardize my grade? What was Lauren thinking? We needed good grades to keep the club. The only item I felt at all comfortable with was the flip-flop thing.

I pulled my phone out of my jeans pocket and dialed Lauren's number, making sure the hair dryer was on high so its roar would drown out my voice. Ryan has a bad habit of eavesdropping. The phone rang twice and then Lauren picked up.

"Hey, Lauren. It's Charlie. I'm in the bathroom so I have to talk fast."

"Gross. What is wrong with you, Charlie? Call me when you're finished."

"No, I'm hiding in the bathroom because . . . well . . . it doesn't matter. Anyway, I've read my initiation list and . . ."

"It's awesome, isn't it?" Lauren interrupted.

"Um . . . here's the thing, Lauren. There are some things on here that I don't think I should do. Has anyone else called you about that?"

"No, Charlie. You're the only one. Everyone else is really excited to be part of the Junior Waves."

"Yeah, I'm excited, too . . . it's just that . . . well . . . I could get in trouble for some of this stuff. Like stealing, for instance."

"It's just Starbucks," Lauren said. "You're not going to go to jail for taking a cookie. Besides, it's so crowded in there after school, no one will ever catch you. Bethany worked that one out with me. And the coolest thing of all is that she's going to be there to watch you do it. Not to brag or anything, but she says I'm doing an awesome job as president."

"But Lauren, I'm not sure I can do this."

There was a long silence on the other end of the phone. At last, she spoke, and her voice was icy cold.

"It's up to you, Charlie. I thought you wanted to be a Junior Wave. I thought you wanted to be one of us. If you do, you have to show your loyalty. But if you don't, well, we'll just have to go on without you."

Ryan pounded on the door again.

"Charles," he shouted. "If you don't get out of there, I'm going to pee right here in the hall."

"Oh, is that Ryan?" Lauren asked. "Tell him I say hi."

And then she hung up.

I stood up, took one last look at the list, tore it up into little tiny pieces and flushed it down the toilet.

I didn't sleep much that night. I kept seeing the list in my head, and when I did, my heart would start to pound. Could I look right into a teacher's eyes and refuse to turn in my homework? Could I swipe something right off the principal's desk? Could I actually steal from Starbucks?

It all came down to one question: How much did I really want to be a Junior Wave? And I guess I wasn't sure.

It Begins

······································

Chapter 12

"Is there something wrong with your foot, Noodle?" GoGo asked the next morning as I came into the kitchen for breakfast. I was wearing one flip-flop and one shoe.

"My heel's been hurting me for a couple of days," I lied, "so I didn't think wearing a shoe would be a good idea."

Wouldn't you know it, my dad walked into the kitchen at that very minute.

"Let me see your foot," he said. "You girls are playing this weekend and we can't have any injuries."

"It's nothing, Dad. I'm sure it will be better by tomorrow. Maybe even by tonight."

"Let's have a look," he persisted, sitting me down and taking my foot in his hands. He pressed on several spots in my heel, which didn't hurt at all, but I faked a little wince, just to make an injury seem real.

"I don't see any swelling," he said. "But just to be sure, we'll ice it when you get home from school. And keep that foot elevated as much as you can in school today. Want me to write a note you can take to the nurse?"

"No, Dad. Honestly, that's not necessary. I'll just wear this flip-flop and it'll be fine."

"Why not just wear two flip-flops?" my dad wanted to know.

"Flip-flops aren't allowed in school," I explained. "But I can get away with one because of my in-injury," I stammered.

Even though he had a tennis lesson to give, he insisted on driving me to school so I wouldn't strain my foot any further. Thankfully, Sammie had already left for school. Otherwise, she would have figured out I was faking it.

As I walked into school, everyone seemed to want to know why I was wearing two different shoes. Including Principal Pfeiffer, who always greets students as they arrive at school.

"Hi, Charlie," he said. "Hope that foot's not going to affect your tournament play. I see you've got a big match against Bryant and Shinoda coming up."

Boy, he really did follow our tennis schedule! I was thinking about how flattering that was, when suddenly, it hit me. Item number three on the list was to bring Lauren something from Principal Pfeiffer's desk. What better time than now? It was a sign that going ahead with initiation was the right decision.

"Principal Pfeiffer," I said. "I hear your son plays tennis. If you like, I could give him a list of some warm-up exercises my sister and I do before a match."

He broke out into a big smile.

"Why, that would be a very kind thing of you to do, Charlie. Thank you."

"No problem," I said. "I think I have some paper in my locker. If I hurry I can go get it right now. I'll leave it on your desk before the bell rings, if that's okay."

"Of course," he said. "Just tell Mrs. Romero that I said for you to go right in."

This was one lucky break. Maybe I could have two of my initiation assignments done before first period even started.

Once inside the hall, I pulled a piece of paper from my notebook, leaned up against the wall and quickly wrote down a list of five warm-up exercises Sammie and I do—basic drills like trunk twisting, diagonal sprints and slides, stuff like that. Then, with that paper in hand, I walked into the school office and found Mrs. Romero at her desk.

"May I help you?" she asked.

"I have this paper for Principal Pfeiffer," I said, aware that my heart was thumping faster than usual. "It's a list of tennis exercises for his son."

"You can hand it to me," she said, coming over to

the counter. "I'll leave it for him."

"Actually, I just saw him and he said that I should personally leave it on his desk."

She looked over her glasses at me, a curious expression on her face.

"He said that?" Did I hear a suspicious tone in her voice . . . or was it just my guilty conscience?

"Yes, he did, Mrs. Romero. He said just those words."

Without answering, she walked over to the gate that separates the waiting area from her desk, and held it open for me. I forced a smile and walked through it, flashing her the paper with the list of drills, in case she thought I was making this all up.

"Thank you, Mrs. Romero," I said.

Gathering up all my nerve, I walked past her and into Mr. Pfeiffer's office. Quickly, my eyes scanned his desk for something I could take. Something that only a principal would have, but that he wouldn't miss if I took it. A banana? No, anyone could have a banana on his desk. A pen? No, that looked like an expensive one. I walked up to his desk and laid the piece of paper down, letting my eyes skim over all the other papers there. Then I saw it, the perfect thing.

It was a card with his name written on it from Frankie's Barber Shop. It was a reminder that he had an appointment for a haircut at 4:30 that day with Frankie himself. I didn't know that bald men had to get their hair cut.

Quickly, I snatched the card off the desk and slid it into my jeans pocket. When I looked up, Mrs. Romero was standing in the doorway, staring at me. I felt myself turning red in the face.

"Young lady, is there something you're looking for?" she asked in a harsh voice.

I couldn't tell if she had seen me pick up the card or not. Maybe I had already slipped it into my pocket by the time she got to the doorway. But maybe I hadn't. Should I confess right there or pretend that nothing had happened? I looked at her face, which had a sour expression on it—but she was a grumpy woman, so that didn't necessarily mean she was ready to accuse me.

Don't be crazy, Charlie. You want to be a Junior Wave, right? So confessing isn't an option.

I took a deep breath and plunged ahead.

"I was just looking for a place to put this paper down," I lied. "I was looking for a place that wouldn't disturb anything on his desk."

It sounded pretty good. I was getting better at this lying business.

Mrs. Romero looked at me for a long minute. I hoped she didn't notice that my hands were shaking. And it felt like my chest was going to explode. Finally, the silence was broken by the morning bell ringing. It startled me so much I almost jumped five feet in the air.

"Very well," she said. "You'd better get to class."

Phew! I practically flew out of the office. By the time I got into the hall, I was drenched in sweat, and it wasn't even hot out. As stressful as that was, I have to confess that I felt a strange excitement at having pulled it off.

On my way to first period, I ran into Brooke in the hall. She was wearing a football helmet on her head, obviously part of her initiation list. We both smiled at each other, exchanging a secret look that only another Junior Wave would understand. That was fun.

My next initiation assignment was to take place during second-period Spanish. Although I was nervous about it, after staring down Mrs. Romero, I was feeling a little more confident about facing Señora Molina and refusing to turn in my homework. I could do this.

When I slid into my desk in Spanish class, Jillian passed me a note.

How's it going? it read.

"Better than you can even imagine," I whispered as she slid into her desk. I noticed she was wearing her clothes inside out.

We always start class by reciting a poem in Spanish, just to get our throats warmed up and our *r*s rolling, or so Señora Molina says. As we did our poem, I could see Sammie's friend Sara on the other side of the class, staring at my foot with the flip-flop. She was frowning. After the poem, Señora Molina asked everyone to pass their homework to the front so she could collect it. We were supposed to write a paragraph describing one of our parents. When she got to the front of my row, Señora Molina glanced over the papers and noticed that mine wasn't there.

"Charlie," she said, "please pass your homework to the front."

"No, thank you," I said.

She stopped and looked up at me.

"What did you say?" she asked.

"Oh," I said. "I meant to say, *No, gracias.*"

I could hear Jillian's giggle behind me.

"Charlie," she said, approaching my desk. "I asked for your homework. Now do you have it or not?"

"I have it, but I can't turn it in, Señora."

"And may I ask why?"

"It's just not good enough yet," I said.

"I'll be the judge of that," she answered briskly. "That's why I'm the teacher and you're the student."

"I'm sorry, Señora Molina," I said, "but I'm just not comfortable turning it in today."

"Do you understand that if you don't turn in your homework, you'll get a zero on the assignment?" she asked me.

"Yes. I mean *sí.*"

"And that this paragraph I assigned you represents your whole week's homework grade?"

I nodded.

"I just don't know why you'd choose to jeopardize your good grade in this class," she said, shaking her head. "I'm very disappointed in you, Charlie."

She moved over to the next row. To my surprise, I felt sudden tears welling up in my eyes. I liked Señora Molina. She was a teacher who really cared that her students did well. And she seemed so confused—or was she hurt?—by my stupid refusal to cooperate. When I glanced over at Jillian, I saw that she was giving me a thumbs-up. I tried to smile and then turned my head away quickly so she wouldn't catch sight of my watery eyes.

Finally, the bell rang and we filed out of class. As I was walking to my locker, Sammie ran up to me.

"What's going on with you?" she demanded. "Sara told me you made a scene in Spanish class."

"Nothing. Why do you think something's going on?"

"Because you're wearing one shoe. Because you're refusing to turn in homework. Because you're acting totally weird. Want me to go on?"

Lauren walked by us.

"Jillian gave me the report. Nicely done," she whispered before she trotted ahead to join Brooke at her locker.

"It's something to do with her, isn't it?" Sammie asked. "What's Lauren doing to you?"

"Is that all you can think about?" I snapped. "Lauren is my friend. We're having fun, if that's okay with you. I think you're just jealous that I'm back with my old friends and I don't need you and your little pals anymore."

"That's low, Charlie, and you know it."

There we were, fighting again. Sammie stomped off without another word, and to my surprise, those tears in my eyes welled up again.

By the time lunch came around, I was in a really bad mood. I was standing at my locker, trying to make sense of the morning, when Spencer walked up. The sight of him cheered me up somewhat.

"Mmmmm," he said. "Smells great in here. Is that pepperoni?"

I blushed.

"I know it's disgusting," I said with a shrug, "but I love cold pizza. My grandmother always puts it in my lunch when there are any leftovers."

"I knew that lady was cool the first time I saw her," he said. "Cold pizza is my favorite thing. Well, except for cold Chinese food."

"You're weird," I said.

"Me? You're the one with the locker that smells like pepperoni!"

I took my lunch bag and handed it to him.

"You can have it. I'm not that hungry."

The stress of the morning was actually making

me a little sick to my stomach.

"Really? Don't make that offer again, Charlie, because I swear, I'll take you up on it."

I handed him the bag and he snatched it from me with a big smile.

"Man, this sure beats cafeteria tacos with ground-up mystery meat," he said.

We headed down the hall and out to the lunch pavilion. Most of the SF2s were already gathered at our table. Lauren got up and met me before I reached the bench.

"Excuse us, Spencer," she said. "We have some private business to discuss."

"No problemo," he said. "I've got some cold pizza to eat."

As soon as he had taken his place at the table, Lauren whispered to me. "It's going great," she said. "What you did in Spanish class was unbelievable. And I see that you're wearing one flip-flop, which is also excellent. Jilly and Brooke are doing great, too."

I reached into my jeans pocket and handed her the haircut appointment card from Principal Pfeiffer's desk.

"Item number three from my list," I said. "Mission accomplished."

Lauren looked at it, then burst out laughing. "Wait until I show this to Bethany," she hooted. "She'll die. So now it's just lifting that cookie from Starbucks and you're done."

"I was thinking . . . how about if we call it quits now?" I said.

"Are you kidding me, Charlie? Bethany is coming to Starbucks to watch you. After that, she'll give us her final permission to have the Initiation Ceremony tonight."

"Wait, I didn't know everything depended on her."

"Well, technically it doesn't," Lauren said. "But she is our sponsor and also the most popular Wave in the whole high school. So I think we should listen to her, don't you? Now come on, let's sit down. We don't want any of the guys to get suspicious."

At the lunch table, I noticed that Brooke was putting three packets of hot sauce on her tacos. She took one bite and started waving her hand in front of her mouth to cool it down. She reached for a cup of water and chugged the whole thing down. Lauren was watching her carefully.

"Wow, I didn't know you liked your food so hot," the General said to her.

Brooke had reached into the cup and pulled out an ice cube. She was holding it to her tongue.

"Ahhh don't" she tried to say. She looked over at Lauren, her eyes watering from the heat inside her mouth.

"Good girl, Brookie," Lauren whispered to her. "Now you're done."

"Me too?" I asked. I thought it couldn't hurt to try one more time.

"You're almost done," Lauren giggled. "Trust me, the best is yet to come."

I wished with all my might that I was done, but Lauren wasn't letting me off the hook. Starbucks lay ahead—and along with it, my first time ever committing an actual crime.

Starbucks

....

Chapter 13

"Charlie, over here," Lauren called out as I made my way across the crowded patio of Starbucks.

Finally, I saw Lauren, standing at the far end with Brooke and Jillian and Bethany. They were each happily sipping a blended drink. Dodging tables and chairs, I crossed the patio and approached their smiling little group. I wasn't smiling. In fact, I felt like throwing up.

"What took you so long to get here?" Lauren asked.

"I even left my last period early so I wouldn't miss this," Bethany said. "And you come strolling in late. I should ding you for this."

"Ding?" I repeated.

"It's a Waves thing. Three dings and you're on

probation. Five dings and you're out. We have a strict moral code."

Right, she would be the one to know about a strict moral code, this girl who is asking me to steal.

"Don't be such a grump, Bethany," Lauren said. "We're here to celebrate, aren't we? This is the last initiation test before we all become Junior Waves."

I looked at Jillian and Brooke. They didn't seem nearly as nervous as I was.

"Aren't you guys scared?" I asked them.

"Of what?" Jillian said. "Drinking a mocha blended? I do that every day."

I looked at Lauren and before I could ask her, she answered the question she knew was on my mind.

"You're the only one who's been asked to take a cookie from Starbucks, Charlie. The other girls have finished their initiation assignments. Remember, Brooke had to do that thing at lunch?"

"Wait a minute," I complained. "Brooke has to eat some hot sauce, and I have to steal? That's not fair! I already stole something off Principal Pfeiffer's desk. That should be enough!"

"Well," Bethany said, "I explained to Lauren that you had farther to go to prove your loyalty, given what happened with Sean and Jared and everything. So we had to make your test a little tougher than Brooke's or Jillian's."

"What about Lily? Is she doing this, too?" I asked.

"Oh no," Lauren said. "All of Lily's assignments

had to do with getting the T-shirts ready in time. That's why she's not here."

"Does she know about this?"

"Charlie," Lauren said, her voice sounding really impatient, "for your information, a president doesn't have to tell the members every little detail."

Oh, so that explained it. I didn't think Lily was the kind of person who'd go along with a plan that involved stealing.

"Now come on, Charlie," Bethany said, checking the time on her phone. "Get this over with. Just walk past the basket, slip a packaged cookie into your pocket, and then get in line and order a Frappuccino. No big deal. We've all done worse things."

Maybe she had, but I hadn't.

Quickly, I walked past the basket that held the cookies. I was so nervous, I felt like my mouth was filled with cotton. Then, in one swift move, I picked one up and slipped it in my pocket. I was literally shaking by the time I got to the front of the line.

"What'll you have, honey?" the man behind the counter asked me.

"One Frappuccino." My voice sounded shaky to me. I wondered if it sounded that way to him, too.

"Want anything to eat with that?"

I shook my head.

Out of the corner of my eye, I could see Lauren and the girls giggling and nodding. Quickly, I looked away from them. Out of the window, I saw a black-and-white police car cruising by. I started to really panic.

"So what do we have again?" Jake asked, snapping my attention back. "Just one Frappuccino?"

I felt a hand grab my shoulder from the back. I wheeled around so fast, it made me dizzy. I honestly thought I was going to faint. This was it. The moment I had been dreading. I knew what I did was wrong, and now I was going to have to pay for it. Why, oh why, did I do it?

It wasn't the police, though. It was Spencer, grinning at me with both of his deep darling dimples showing. I was never so glad to see a friendly face.

"They told me I'd find you here," he said. "Looks like I arrived just in time."

Oh no! Did he know, too? "In time for wh-wh-what?" I stammered.

"To buy you a Starbucks," he grinned.

"Why?"

"Because you gave me your lunch. And because I think us guys who love cold pizza need to stick together."

"Come on, kids. You're holding up the line," Jake said, a little irritated now. "What do you have?"

"One Frappuccino," Spencer said.

"And a chocolate-chip cookie," I added, quickly pulling the cookie out of my pocket, hoping no one noticed. Suddenly, I felt so light and free I wanted to dance or sing or shout.

Spencer reached into his wallet and pulled out a

ten dollar bill, enough money to pay for both the drink AND the cookie.

Let me just say this now—and you can go ahead and think I'm crazy if you want to. But I actually believe that Spencer's arrival right at that very moment was a sign. I don't know from whom or from what. But I do know that he arrived just in time to stop me from doing something that I knew was wrong. Maybe if he hadn't come, I wouldn't have stolen the cookie, anyway. I hope that's true. But he did come, and was I ever glad to see him.

Lauren wasn't.

When I went back to the girls, Lauren glared at me and said, "He ruined everything."

"It wasn't my fault he showed up," I said. "I didn't ask him to."

"What matters is if Charlie finishes her initiation," Jillian said. "Did she, Lauren?"

Lauren looked at Bethany, who just shrugged.

"You're the president," she said. "Presidents have to make tough decisions."

By the time Lauren made her decision, I had already joined Spencer at a table on the patio, and we were sharing the best chocolate-chip cookie I'd ever had.

The Ceremony

....

Chapter 14

"I've decided to let you in," Lauren's text had said. "Meet on the beach at sunset."

Spencer watched my face as I popped the last bit of cookie into my mouth and read the text. I broke out into a big smile.

"Looks like you got some good news," he said, and waited for me to say something. But I just nodded and changed the subject.

I was relieved. I guess Lauren thought I had proved my loyalty. Now I wouldn't have to do any more of those horrible initiation assignments. I could just look forward to the ceremony on the beach, where we'd be sworn in as sisters forever, and my life as a Junior Wave would begin for real.

When I got home, Sammie was lying on her bed, flipping through some pictures on her phone.

"How's it going with Sara and the makeover?" I asked as I slipped off my school clothes and changed into a pair of clean jeans.

"Why'd you bring that up?" she asked without looking up.

"Because I assume those are the pictures you're looking at. Am I right?"

She looked up from her phone long enough to give me a crabby look.

"How come you get to ask all the questions?" she said. "I've got one for you. Why won't you tell me what's going on with you?"

"Nothing's going on."

"Fine, then nothing's going on with Sara, either."

"Sammie," my dad called from the kitchen. "Come set the table. And help GoGo with dinner."

"I gotta go," she said, putting her phone back into the side pocket of her purse and zipping it up. We both keep our phones zipped up in the side pockets of our bags so they're out of nosy Ryan's sight. He thinks it's a riot to read our texts and make fun of them. He believes texts should just be for making plans: "meet you at seven," that kind of thing. So when we say "love you" or "can't wait to see you" or "sleep tight," he thinks it's hilarious.

After Sammie left, I glanced out the window and saw Lauren and Brooke arriving at the club. Lily was following behind them, carrying what looked like a laundry bag stuffed with clothes. I saw her walk out toward the beach, while Lauren and Brooke stayed behind talking to each other. From their body language, I could tell something was wrong. In twenty seconds, there was an urgent knock at my bedroom door. When I opened it, Brooke was crying and Lauren looked furious.

"Charlie," Brooke said tearfully. "I need to borrow your charger. My phone's dead."

"A certain somebody forgot to charge her phone," Lauren said. "I wonder who."

I went to my dresser and took the charger out of the plug in the wall.

"Here," I said, handing it to Brooke. "Problem solved."

Brooke looked at the charger and burst into more tears.

"This is for the old model," she said. "It won't work on my phone."

"I didn't think anyone still had an old phone like yours," Lauren said to me.

"I'm getting a new one for my birthday." That wasn't true. In fact, my dad had already made it clear that if I wanted a new phone, I was going to have to babysit and earn the money myself.

"What's the big deal, Brooke?" I asked, stepping aside so they could come in. "We don't need to talk on the phone during the ceremony."

"I need the phone to play the song," she said. "Our song. I stayed up half the night listening to a million songs, and I finally picked the perfect one that describes us. It's called "We Are the Champions" by this old band named King."

"Queen," I said. "The band is called Queen."

Brooke's eyes grew wide. "You know the song?"

"Sure. It's on the playlist that Sammie and I listen to before every tournament. It gets us psyched up to win."

"So do you have it on your phone?" Lauren asked. "Yup."

Brooke threw her arms around me.

"While you two are hugging it out, maybe Charlie can get out her phone." Lauren sighed. "Nevermind. I'll get it."

"In my bag, on the dresser. Zipper pocket—"

"I know . . . the side zipper pocket." Lauren finished my sentence before I could. "Where you and Sammie hide your phones so Ryan can't get them. We've been best friends for almost two months, Charlie. I know everything about you."

Actually, she didn't know everything. I hide my phone in the left-side zipper pocket. Sammie hides hers in the right side. But this was no time to get into details. We had an initiation ceremony to attend.

Lauren grabbed my phone and we headed out to the beach. Lily and Jillian were waiting for us at the end of the jetty. The sky was starting to turn a darker shade of blue, which meant that we only had a few minutes before sunset. We got started right away.

"I brought us low-fat chocolate mocha Frappuccinos," Jillian said proudly, pulling five bottles out of a Starbucks bag and setting them down in a circle. "You won't believe this, but I actually called Neela for a suggestion, and she told me this is what the ancient Aztec people used in their ceremonies."

"Wow, I didn't know they had Starbucks back then," Brooke said.

"They didn't. At least, I don't think they did," Jillian answered. "But Neela said they had cacao beans, which is what you make chocolate from. And when the Aztecs celebrated, they brought the kings cacao beans as special gifts. So that's why I picked the chocolate Frappuccinos and not the caramel ones."

I thought it was very sweet that Jillian had done that much research. And that Brooke had stayed up late looking for just the right song. Everyone was taking this very seriously.

Next, Lily opened the laundry bag and pulled out five white shirts that belonged to her dad. She handed each of us one. Her dad is very tall, so the shirts looked like dresses on us. Then she reached into the bag and pulled out a whole bunch of bright orange flowers.

"These are marigolds," she said. "Neela helped me pick them especially for tonight."

She reached into the bag and pulled out five turquoise headbands.

"I thought we could each put one of these in our hair," she said, "and tuck a few marigolds into it. Then our heads will be covered with turquoise and orange, the colors of the Junior Waves."

We slipped the headbands on, and arranged the flowers in each other's hair.

"Look at us." Lily beamed. "We look so good!"

The sun was lower in the sky by then, and the sea breeze was getting stronger. A few gulls and pelicans circled overhead, like they usually do when twilight starts to fall. Lauren asked us to gather in a circle and sit down. She told us to just sit for a moment and listen to the waves crashing against the jetty. Then she turned the volume up on my phone, placed it in the center of the circle and played "We Are the Champions." Lily, Brooke, and I knew the words and sang along. By the middle of the song, everyone knew the chorus and we sang together at the top of our lungs.

We are the champions
No time for losers
'Cause we are the champions of the world.

When the song ended, Jillian passed out the Frappuccinos and Lauren officially began the ceremony.

"We are gathered here to become Junior Wave sisters," Lauren began. "We are going to take a pledge that we will share everything and be loyal to each other forever. Each of us must be tested. The test that I, your president, have created is called TRUTH and TRUST."

"Uh-oh, it sounds hard," Brooke said. "This isn't like school, is it?"

"You don't have to know anything special to pass this test," Lauren answered.

"Phew," Brooke whispered. "I thought it was going to be like geography questions or something."

"The trust test will consist of two parts," Lauren said. "In the truth part, you must share a secret with the group, something you have never shared with anyone. In the trust part, you must answer a question from the group. You must answer truthfully and honestly until the group is satisfied."

Lauren reached down to pick up a piece of beach driftwood that she had brought with her.

"This is our talking stick," she said. "When you

have the stick, you must share. When I tell you to pass it, you must do so."

Lauren held the talking stick out and gave it to Lily first.

"Lily March," she said. "Will you please share your secret? You can trust us."

Lily held the stick and squirmed a little bit. This wasn't easy.

"Any kind of secret?" she asked.

Lauren nodded. "Something you have never shared before."

"Okay, here goes," Lily said. "When I was born, I was very premature and weighed a pound and a half. They didn't think I was going to live. I had a twin brother, but he didn't live."

"Wow, I didn't know that, Lilykins," Brooke said.

"That's why they call it a secret," Lauren said. "Thank you for sharing, Lily."

Lily handed the stick to Brooke.

"Okay," Brooke giggled. "My secret is . . . um . . . that I don't have any secrets."

She passed the stick to Lauren, who wouldn't take it.

"Sorry, that doesn't cut it, Brooks. If you want to pass TRUTH and TRUST and be one of the Junior Wave sisters, you have to do better. Now, do you want to share a secret or not?"

"Do I have to?"

"Yes, Brooke. You do."

"Okay, my dad isn't my real dad," Brooke blurted out all of a sudden. "My real dad left my mom before I was born."

No one said anything. She handed the stick back to Lauren like it was a hot potato. Next, it came to me. I wanted to trust these girls who meant so much to me. So I swallowed hard and told the truth.

"My dad lost his last job," I said. "We had to move to the Sporty Forty because it was the only place we could afford to live."

I thought I heard a couple of the girls gasp. Lily reached out and touched me gently on the arm.

"That was brave," was all she said.

I handed the stick to Jillian.

"When my parents aren't home," she said, "I used to go to their room and look at this book of photos of naked people. But I think they found out, because now it's gone."

Jillian gave the stick to Lauren. "Now it's your turn, Madame President."

Lauren held the stick. She closed her eyes and seemed to be reaching deep down for a secret. At last she spoke.

"One time, I stole an eye shadow from the makeup counter at Bloomingdales."

"What color?" Brooke asked.

"It doesn't matter," Lily whispered. "That's not the point."

"Terra cotta bronze," Lauren said softly, putting

down the talking stick. "It didn't stay on, either."

Everyone laughed. I was feeling so close to these girls. It's really powerful how sharing your innermost secrets can make you feel so connected to other people. Oddly, I thought of Sammie. This was exactly how she had described Truth Tellers. I remember her saying how "powerful and raw" the experience was. Sitting out there on the jetty with my friends, I was able to allow the powerful feeling of sharing to fill me with awe.

"So when is the swearing in?" Brooke asked. "We should do it before the sun completely goes down because it's getting cold out here."

"We have only completed the truth part," Lauren said. "We will now begin part two, trust. I will ask each of you a question. You must answer truthfully, no matter how hard it is. We have to trust that we can be completely open with each other."

Lauren handed the talking stick to Lily first.

"Lily March," she said. "How old were you when you got your first period, and where were you?"

"Eleven," Lily answered. "In my cabin at summer camp. After I told my counselor, she must have told someone else, because all the boys found out."

"What did they do?" I asked.

"Teased me. Squirted packets of ketchup on my clothes. It was awful. They all had to write letters of apology. That was even worse."

I reached out and put my hand on her arm.

"It sounds so embarrassing," I said.

"Now your question, Brooke," Lauren said, handing her the talking stick. "Have you ever met your real father?"

"Do I have to answer that?" Brooke said.

"Yes, to prove that you trust us," Lauren told her.

"Okay," Brooke said slowly and carefully. "I met him once. He appeared out of nowhere about three years ago."

"Did he say where he'd been?" Jillian asked.

"Here and there."

"Brooke," Lauren said. "You have to give truthful answers."

"That is the truth."

"Not the whole truth. This is about trusting us with the whole truth."

Brooke hesitated. She looked down at the talking stick, running her fingers over the smooth surface of the driftwood.

"Okay, he had been in jail," she said. "He went to jail for selling drugs. He's out on probation now, and wants to see me, but I don't want to see him."

Everyone was quiet. I was sure no one else in the Sporty Forty had a dad who'd been in jail. It made my dad losing his job seem like nothing.

"That was really brave of you to confess," I told her. She seemed glad to hear that.

"Your turn, Jillian," Lauren said.

Jillian took the stick and waited for her question.

"What is the most embarrassing thing that's ever happened to you?"

"The first time I ever kissed a boy, I wasn't sure what to do. So I pressed my lips against his really hard like they do in the movies. I knocked him down and he got a bloody nose."

"I never heard about this," Brooke said. "Who was it?"

"Um . . . it was . . ." She hesitated, then blurted out the truth. "It was Nicky."

"*Nicky*? As in *my brother* Nicky?" Brooke couldn't believe what she was hearing.

Jillian nodded sheepishly.

"He's not supposed to go around kissing my friends," Brooke said. "Wait until I talk to him about this. I'm going to tell Mom and Dad, too. He will be so grounded."

"You can't do that, Brooke," I said. "Whatever we say here, stays here."

I felt a little guilty stealing that line from Truth Tellers. It was their motto and not ours, but it was a good one.

"We have to move on, anyway," Lauren said. "It's getting too cold out here. Charlie, you're next."

She took the talking stick from Jillian and handed it to me.

"This is your question," she began. "Can you tell us one thing you promised never to tell?"

That caught me totally by surprise.

"Wait a minute," I said. "I thought these questions were supposed to be about *us*."

"This is about you," Lauren said. "It's about how much you trust us—not only with your own secrets but with someone else's."

"Okay," I said. "My mom colors her hair."

"Well of course she does," Lauren snapped. "All our moms do. Come on, Charlie. You can do better than that. It's not fair—everyone else has shared a real secret. You're going to have to trust us, too."

Of course, the first thing that popped into my mind was the most recent secret that had been shared with me—the secret of Sara Berlin's terrible protruding ears. But I couldn't tell that.

But I had nothing else to say. And everyone was staring at me.

"I . . . I . . . do have one, but I can't tell you. I promised."

"If we can't trust you to answer the question truthfully, how can we trust you to be one of us?" Lauren asked.

The only thing I could do was repeat what I had already said.

"But I made a promise." I could hear myself saying it more weakly.

"Isn't the promise you made to us more important?" Lauren asked.

I looked at the faces of my friends. They were all waiting for an answer and part of me felt I owed them one. It couldn't have been easy for Brooke to tell us that her real father had been in jail. Or for Jillian to confess that she had kissed Brooke's brother—and given him a bloody nose. Or for Lily to say that her twin brother had died at birth. All of that took a lot of bravery.

But then I thought about Sara Berlin and how her eyes had filled with tears when she even tried to talk about her ears. It had caused her such pain, for so many years. She had trusted all of us with a secret, a secret we promised to keep.

"Charlie, we're waiting," Lauren said.

I sat there listening to the waves crash on the rocks. Out over the ocean, I could make out the silhouette of a brown pelican flying low over the water. I watched as he circled around, and then suddenly dived into the water. When he came up, he had a fish in his beak. I could see the poor little fish thrashing, trying to get free, but the pelican held on tight.

As I sat in the circle, the unanswered question looming over me like a black cloud, I felt like that poor fish, squirming and wriggling, trying to find a way to break free to safety.

Overheard

....

Chapter 15

"I don't think Charlie should have to answer if she doesn't want to," Lily said at last, breaking the silence.

I felt a huge wave of relief sweeping over me. But it didn't last long.

"I don't think that's fair, Lily," Brooke said. "Each of us answered our question. Why should Charlie get off without answering hers?"

"Because her question involves another person," Lily said.

"Oh, and my story didn't?" Jillian said. "I seem to remember spilling the beans about a certain someone's brother named Nick."

"I still can't believe you kissed him," Brooke groaned.

"I have made my decision," Lauren said. "Charlie,

we've all shared difficult things. That's what will bond us as sisters. You need to show that you trust us and answer the question. Waves, if you agree with me, raise your hand."

Everyone raised their hand but Lily. There it was—the decision. No more stalling. If I wanted to be in the Junior Waves, I had to answer the question. I hated to. But I also couldn't stand the thought of everyone being in the club but me. I hated the idea of not sitting with them at the football games. Most of all, I never wanted to feel left out again.

So I took a breath and plunged in.

"Remember the other day, when Sammie wouldn't let us in my room?" I began. "Well, it's because she was in there with Alicia and Sara Berlin, trying to come up with a new look for Sara. They were doing different things with her hair, and then taking before and after pictures."

"So what's the big secret?" Jillian asked. "You can see a makeover every day on TV."

"They were trying to help Sara cover up something that she's ashamed of," I explained, still trying to respect her privacy and not mention the real problem. I stopped, hoping they would leave it at that. I should have known better.

"What's she so ashamed of?" Lauren asked.

I hesitated.

"Her ears," I said at last.

"What's wrong with her ears?" Brooke said. "Is

she like missing them or something?"

"They protrude," I answered. "A lot. Kids have been teasing her about it ever since she was little. Calling her Dumbo and stuff."

"I knew this boy in my Sunday school class whose ears stuck out so far they looked like tea cups," Jillian said. "We called him Mr. Potato Head until the teacher overheard us and sent us to have a talk with Pastor Clarke. We got in big trouble. He called our parents and everything."

"Sara says she's suffered with that kind of teasing all her life," I said. "It's really affected her self-esteem."

"Of course it would," Lily said. "Were Sammie and Alicia able to help her?"

"They're working on it," I said. "They've tried telling her to forget the teasing; that her real friends like her for who she is, not the way she looks."

Lauren laughed. "Yeah, right."

"So they took pictures of her the way she really looks with her hair pulled back and her ears sticking out," I continued, trying to ignore Lauren's remark. "Then they put things like scarves and headbands and hats on her and took another picture, to see if it looks good."

"So there are pictures of her real ears and everything?" Lauren asked. "Could we see them?"

"Why do you need to see them? I told you the truth."

"Oh, I don't need to," Lauren said. "It would just be

fun. You know, like seeing a bearded lady at the circus. It's interesting in a creepy kind of way."

I handed the talking stick back to Lauren. I'm sure she didn't intend to compare Sara to a bearded lady in the circus, but even if she hadn't meant to, it sounded pretty harsh. I was done with this conversation. Fortunately, the orange streaks in the sky were dimming and night was quickly approaching.

"It's really late," Brooke said. "We should hurry up and do Lauren's question. Who gets to ask it?"

"I will," Lily said. "I have a good one. Lauren, what is the one thing you want most in the world?"

I was amazed that Lauren didn't even stop to think about it. The answer was on the tip of her tongue.

"To be the most popular girl in high school," she said.

"Why not the most popular girl in middle school?" Jillian asked.

"Obviously, because I already am. I want to be just like Bethany," she went on. "She has a hot boyfriend, a closet full of great clothes, and a ton of friends. My mom says she thinks she's got Prom Queen in the bag."

Suddenly, my phone, which was still sitting in the middle of our circle, rang. I looked at who was calling.

"It's Ryan," I said.

"Tell him I say hi," Lauren squealed.

"Where are you, Charles?" Ryan said, without bothering to say hello. "Jillian's mom is here to pick her up and so is Lily's dad. By the way, Lauren's very hot cousin is here to take her home. Anyway, they all want you guys back immediately, if not sooner."

"We'll be right there," I said. "We're almost done."

"Done with what?"

Oops.

"Uh . . . uh . . . nothing."

"So let me get this straight," he said. "You're almost done doing nothing? How does that work exactly?"

"It's totally logical, Ryan."

"Okay, if you say so. Oh, and don't bother coming home," he said. "I'll have the ambulance come and take you directly to the nuthouse."

Then he did his crazy zombie laugh and hung up.

"We better get going," I said.

"First, everyone stand up and raise your right hand," Lauren commanded. We did. "Do you swear to stay true to the sisters of the Junior Waves?" she asked. "And to always remember this night?"

"I do," we answered in unison.

"Then I now declare us officially initiated. Congratulations to us all!"

We took off our white shirts and headbands and packed them into the laundry bag. Walking back along the sand, everyone was quiet. I think the ceremony had affected us all in different ways. There was a lot to think about.

By the time we reached the deck, my dad had come out of the clubhouse and was standing next to Bethany.

"I assumed you'd be back by dinnertime," he said.

"We were just hanging out on the beach," I answered.

"After dark? Does that sound like good judgment? Because it doesn't to me."

"Go easy on them, Coach," Bethany said. "I did the same kind of stuff when I was their age. And look how I turned out!"

"I'm going inside," my dad said. "And Charlie, be more considerate next time. Ryan, come with me. It's your night to do dishes."

"I asked your mom if I could come along to pick you up," Bethany told Lauren after Brooke and Jillian had left. "She went inside the club to get something. So, how did it go? I'm dying to find out."

"It was amazing," Lily said.

"Not to brag or anything," Lauren added, "but I think I conducted a perfect initiation ceremony."

"It was so powerful and raw," I agreed, feeling pretty proud of those words.

"We shared deep secrets," Lily said. "We're so close now."

Bethany's face lit up.

"Like what?" she said. "I love deep secrets?"

"We can't say," I told her. "We took an oath."

Bethany laughed.

"Charlie, you seem to forget who you're talking to. It's me, Bethany. Remember? The one who helped you start your little club. Let me remind you that you owe this all to me, and I want to know what was going on out there."

"We can't say," Lily said. "And actually, it wasn't even all that interesting."

"You're lying," Bethany snapped. "Since when are *powerful* and *raw* not interesting? Lauren, if these other girls won't tell me what was going on, I assume you will . . . after all I've done for you."

"Sorry, Beth, I can't," Lauren said.

"Fine," Bethany said. "You girls are impossible. Let's just get in the car and I'll take you home. You need a lift, Lily?"

"Thanks, but my dad's waiting outside."

Lily and I gave each other a big hug.

"Charlie," my dad yelled from inside, "come in here and help Ryan dry the pots and pans."

"Got to go," I said. "Thanks for a wonderful night. See you tomorrow, Bethany."

"You will?"

"Yeah, at the football game. We're sitting with you guys, remember?"

"Oh right, we're babysitting the middle-schoolers."

"You just wait and see how cool we are," Lauren said to her. "I promise, you're going to take those words back."

I went into the kitchen and picked up a dishtowel.

Ryan was standing at the sink, attacking a frying pan with a scouring pad.

"These pots are murder to get clean," Ryan said. "Sammie made herself an omelet, but she left most of it stuck to the pan. I can't wait until Mom gets back and teaches her how to cook without making a total mess."

When he was finished, I dried the frying pan and walked past the counter to put it away in the drawer underneath. I noticed Lauren's notebook sitting on top of the counter. I knew it was hers—you couldn't miss it because it's hot pink and covered in silver-and-black zebra stickers. Zebras are her favorite animal.

"Oh, Lauren forgot her notebook," I said. "Maybe I can catch her. I'll be right back, Ry."

I picked it up and ran outside, hoping she and Bethany hadn't driven off yet. When I approached the gate, I heard their voices in the parking lot. For some reason, and I can't tell you exactly why, I stopped and listened rather than pushing the gate open. Maybe I suspected what I was going to hear. Or maybe I'm just a big snoop. In any case, this is what I heard.

"And we all wore white shirts and sang *We Are the Champions* and then told each other our deepest secrets," Lauren was saying.

"Like what?" Bethany whispered.

"I swore I wouldn't tell," Lauren said.

"Just tell me one."

"If I do, can I come to your party?"

"Okay, but you better make it a good one then."

"Can the other girls come, too?"

"Depends how juicy it is. Now, spill it."

Lauren lowered her voice to whisper. I leaned closer to the gate so I could make out her words.

"How's this?" she said. "Brooke's dad isn't her real dad. Her real dad was in jail for selling drugs and just got out."

"Seriously?"

That did it. I couldn't just stand there and let this happen! I pushed open the gate and there was Lauren, leaning on her mom's car. Bethany was standing so close to her, they could have been hugging.

"Lauren!" I yelled. "What do you think you're doing?"

She whirled around, and her face froze in shock.

"Charlie! What are you doing here?" she cried.

"I live here. And I overheard what you were saying."

"What did you hear?"

"Enough to know that you're telling Bethany our secrets. We took an oath, Lauren. It was *your* oath. I can't believe you're breaking it."

Bethany came over and threw her gorgeous arm around me. I shook it off.

"Don't touch me," I said.

"Calm down. Lauren hardly told me anything. Just a little tidbit."

"That's not true," I shouted. I was so mad I was

shaking. "I heard her tell you about Brooke."

"That was just one tiny little thing," Lauren said. "I didn't tell her anything else, did I, Beth?"

"Well, it's not a tiny thing to Brooke," I snarled. "How would you feel if someone told your deepest secret, just like it was nothing?"

"I'd feel fine," Lauren answered. "Watch." Then turning to Bethany, she said, "I stole an eye shadow from Bloomingdales."

"What color?" Bethany asked.

"Terra cotta bronze."

"Nice, but a little too shimmery," was all Bethany had to say.

I couldn't believe what I was hearing.

"Lauren, what you've just done goes against the whole idea of our trust ceremony," I said. "We're sisters. We have to trust one another, to be true to each other."

"Listen up, Charlie Diamond. I *am* being true to the group!" Now Lauren was yelling. "All I did was tell Bethany one little thing, and in case you didn't realize, it was for the good of the group. I got us all invited to her party Saturday night. That's not called revealing a secret, Charlie. That's called leadership."

"Whoa there, girlfriend," Bethany said. "When did I say *everyone* could come?"

Lauren gave her a smoldering look, and Bethany got the message.

"Okay," she said. "You're all invited. But you have

to leave after the hat throwing."

"See?" Lauren said to me. "No one got hurt. Bethany's never going to tell anyone about Brooke, are you, Beth?"

Bethany held up her hand in the Girl Scout salute.

"Not a peep," she said. "Scout's honor."

"And we all get to go to the party," Lauren said matter-of-factly. "None of the girls will ever know about this, unless you tell them. Can we trust you not to tell, Charlie?"

Wait a minute! Since when did this become about *me* not telling? I wasn't the one who proved she can't keep a secret.

"I don't like what happened here tonight," I said. "I don't feel good about it."

"It's really not as awful as you're making it out to be," Bethany said. "It was just a few words, and words don't mean anything. So why don't you go inside and chill. Everything's going to look different tomorrow."

"Tomorrow, as in the football game," Lauren said to me. "Oh, and did I tell you, Spencer asked if he could sit with us."

"With me or with us?"

"With you, of course. I told him he couldn't since he's not a Junior Wave. But because I'm looking out for you, I said I'd sit you at the end of our row so he can be next to you. He seemed pretty happy with that."

What was I supposed to say to that? Everything's okay now? Let's just forgive and forget?

"Come on, girls," Mrs. Wadsworth called, walking up to the car. "I have a hair appointment I don't want to be late for."

Lauren and Bethany got into the car. As they backed up and slowly pulled out onto Pacific Coast Highway, Lauren rolled down the window, waved at me and shouted, "Junior Waves forever!"

Yeah, right.

Forgive and Forget

....

Chapter 16

"You don't look so good," Sammie said as I climbed into bed that night.

"Thanks," I answered. "Way to build a girl's confidence."

"Having trouble with your new friends, maybe?" she said sarcastically. "What a surprise."

"Everything's fine," I lied. "Or will be, anyway."

I reached over and turned out the light, but tired as I was, I couldn't fall asleep. My mind was racing and my thoughts were all jumbled up. I couldn't stop thinking about how great the day had been, how close I had felt to everyone, and finally how crushing it was to feel like Lauren had betrayed us. But then, maybe she hadn't, my mind argued back. Maybe I was just being dramatic. All she did was trade a little information for the good of the group. Now we'd not only get to go to the football game, but to a high school party as well. On the other hand, my mind retorted, Lauren had broken her solemn oath and that was not easy to forget.

I was like a pancake, flipping from one side of the argument to the other . . . and flipping from my stomach to my back, from my back to my stomach.

"It's pretty hard to fall asleep with you thrashing around like that," Sammie said.

"I can't sleep."

"It's Lauren, isn't it?" Sammie said, flicking on the light. "I bet now that they got their club charter, she wants you out of the group. I told you this would happen."

"That's not it at all," I said. "Not even close. I'm just a little nervous. I have a lot on my mind."

"Nervous about your big Junior Wave debut tomorrow night at the football game?" Sammie said.

"Yeah, that must be what it is," I said.

"Honestly, Charlie, you're turning into one of those girls."

I flicked off the light. Sammie sat up and flicked it back on.

"What now?" I asked. "Did you think of some other terrible comment to make about me?"

"Nope, just forgot my retainer," she said. She got up and went to the bathroom. "It's not in here," she called.

"I think I saw it on the coffee table," I called back.

"Oh yeah," she said, emerging from the bathroom. "I took it out when I was watching TV."

She padded into the living room, and came back with her retainer in.

"I don't know what's wrong with me," she said. "I'm forgetting everything—my retainer, my lunch. Oh, by the way, I also forgot to give you a message from Etta."

"The girl with the green hair? I like her."

"Well, apparently, for some mysterious reason, she likes you, too. She's giving a demonstration tomorrow at lunch and she told me to invite you. She's put together a mixtape of her favorite electronic music and is going to play it with a laser show she's designing."

"Sounds cool," I said.

"Yup. Breaking news, Charlie. The SF2s aren't the only ones who are cool. Some of the rest of us are okay, too."

"I know that."

"Do you?"

Sammie got back in bed and flicked off the light. It was quiet for a while. I just lay there wishing I could talk to her like we used to do, to tell her what happened that night, how confused I was feeling—about Lauren, about Bethany, about myself.

"Sammie," I whispered after a few minutes. "I'm sorry I ditched you the other night. I'm going to try to be a better sister . . . a better person."

I waited for her answer, hoping for her total forgiveness. But all I got was silence. She was already asleep.

When I got to school the next morning, Lily was waiting for me at my locker.

"Here it is," she grinned, handing me a plastic bag. "Open it up. I'm giving you the first one."

Inside was my very own Junior Waves T-shirt.

"Didn't they turn out great?" she beamed. "Do you have some orange shoes for tonight?"

"Nikes," I said.

"Oh, those really bright orange ones with the pink laces? I love those. They're perfect. I haven't seen the other girls yet, so they'll get their shirts at lunch. We can make plans then about how we're getting to the game."

"Just text me what you guys decide," I told her. "I have plans at lunch."

"You're not eating with us?"

"I'm going to an event in Ms. Carew's room. A friend of Sammie's is performing, and I want to be there for her."

"That's nice," Lily said. "By the way, did you get

the text from Lauren this morning?"

"Yup," I said, even though I already knew the news. "Seems we're all invited to Bethany's party on Saturday."

Lily gave me a hug.

"It's been a good week for the Junior Waves," she said as she bounced off down the hall. As I headed off to homeroom, I wished I felt like bouncing, but the events of the night before were still weighing heavily on my mind.

One good thing did happen that morning, though. Spencer Ballard passed me a note in homeroom that said, *Save the seat next to you tonight. I'll bring cold pizza.* I hurriedly shoved the note in my bag before Mr. Boring saw it.

I couldn't help it but my mind started to wander. I thought of our ceremony and almost teared up. So much good had happened. I shouldn't let the argument with Lauren and Bethany ruin it. We all make mistakes. I probably made one by telling Sara's secret. I for sure made one when I ditched Sammie the other night. Lauren made one in sharing one of our secrets with Bethany. But as GoGo always says, human beings make mistakes. That's what makes us human.

Forgive and forget, she says. *Just resolve to do better. That's all anyone can do.*

At lunch, I went to Ms. Carew's room. Etta had set up turntables at the front and Ms. Carew had shoved the desks back and scattered a bunch of big pillows on the floor. About fifteen or twenty kids were there, some leaning on pillows, some sitting cross-legged on the floor. I knew a lot of them from Truth Tellers, but there were some new faces, too.

"Welcome, Charlie," Ms. Carew said. I could tell she was trying not to look surprised to see me there. "Take a seat anywhere."

Sammie hadn't arrived yet. Sara was sitting on the floor, leaning back against a pillow, her long legs with her black lace-up boots stretched out in front of her.

"Hi, Sara," I said, flopping down next to her. "How are things?"

"Looking up," she said. "I'm working on my courage."

Again, that horrible pang of guilt shot through my whole body. She was such a nice girl, working so hard to feel good about herself. Why did I have to go and open my big mouth?

Forgive and forget, Charlie. Just resolve to do better. Remember?

I gave Sara my best smile.

"You're looking great," I said to her. "Courage looks good on you."

"Really?" she said, smiling happily. "Wow, Charlie, that means a lot."

The next thing I saw was the most shocking thing

ever. Sammie came walking in, and directly behind her was none other than Lauren Wadsworth.

"Well, it's nice to see you, Lauren," Ms. Carew said, again trying not to look surprised. "And of course, you too, Sammie."

They both headed over to us. Sammie sat down on the pillow next to me, and Lauren actually sat down next to her. I gave her a look as if to say, *What are you doing here?*

"Lilykins said you were here," she whispered to me.

"So you just came to see me?"

"Kind of," she said. "I had to do something for Bethany. Can you believe it? She gave me one last initiation assignment. At least this one didn't involve any clucking. Anyway, I had to come over to this building, so I thought I'd stop by."

A lot more people came into the room, so we had to squeeze in very close together. Sammie shifted uncomfortably.

"You guys are crowding me," she complained. "I don't have room for my elbows."

"Hand your bags over to me," Lauren said to Sammie and me. "I'll take them over by the door to give us more room."

We handed over our stuff to her, and she high-stepped across the bodies on the floor to the hallway door, arranging our stuff in a neat pile on the floor. Ms. Carew had closed the blinds and lowered the lights so the room was mostly dark. Before Lauren could make her way back to us, Etta flipped on a machine that cast green lasers around the room, and then turned on the music. The lasers flashed in time with the beat of the music.

I looked over at Lauren. I could just barely see her in the darkness, but I motioned for her to come back. She gave me a sign that she'd just stay where she was.

The show lasted about twenty minutes. If I told you it was my kind of music, I'd be lying. It was pretty strange, but the lasers created a cool effect in the darkness. I was glad the room was too crowded for people to dance. The Truth Tellers kind of dancing—no steps and a lot of intense swaying and arm flinging—made me incredibly uncomfortable, especially with Lauren there.

After the show, I went up to Etta and congratulated her. I stayed to help Sammie and Ms. Carew push the chairs back into place for our fifth period class. When we were finished, we stepped out into the hall. Lauren was waiting for us, holding both our bags.

"Forget something?" she said, holding our stuff out to us.

"What is wrong with me this week?" Sammie said. "Next thing you know, I'll forget my name."

Lauren laughed and handed Sammie back her bag.

"Here you go," she said. "Oh, and just in case you forget, it's Samantha, but everyone calls you Sammie."

Sammie nodded. I could tell she thought it was funny, but she wasn't about to give Lauren the satisfaction of laughing at her joke.

I hurried down the hall to my locker to get my English book. Lauren followed me.

"Okay, truth time," she said, walking beside me. "I thought that music thing, or whatever Miss Green Hair calls it, was ridiculous. But I wanted to hang out with you today at lunch, to show you there are no hard feelings. The football game will be so incredible tonight, I don't want anything to ruin it."

I didn't answer, so she went on.

"Did you see the shirts? Aren't they the best? Here's the plan. We're going to meet at the snack stand at the field at six thirty. If you need a ride, we can pick you up."

"That's okay. My dad will drop me off."

"Good, but wear a jacket over your shirt. After we're all together, we'll take our jackets off and make a grand turquoise-and-orange entrance. Bethany says we can sit in the row right above The Waves. Everyone is going to notice us."

It did sound pretty terrific. Lauren was working really hard to make this a fantastic night for all of us. I relaxed a little. *Forgive and forget,* I told myself.

"Do you think anyone will think we're high school kids?"

"Fingers crossed," she giggled. Reaching out to give me a hug, she whispered, "This is going to be so cool," before she ran off to her class.

I got my English books out of my locker and hurried back to class before the bell rang. Sammie was just returning from her locker, and we almost bumped into each other.

"I guess on the list of things you're forgetting, one of them is to look where you're going," I said, in a friendly kind of way. She didn't laugh. "Listen, Sams," I said. "I'm really sorry I've been ignoring you. I've been a lousy sister. But I'll be better. I want things to be okay with us again."

"Easy for you to say," she said. "You weren't the one who got ditched. We had a tradition, Charlie, and you blew it off for something that was more important to you."

"I'm so sorry," I said. "Can't we forgive and forget? Like GoGo says."

"I don't know," she said. "I'll have to work on the forgiving part. The forgetting part is coming easy, though. My head has stopped working completely."

"Just because you forgot where you put your retainer?"

"That's not all. I just went to text dad and it took me forever to find my phone. Turns out I put it in the left zipper pocket this morning. I never do that. Maybe I need to eat more fish. They say it's brain food."

"You've got a great brain, Sams."

"Don't butter me up," she said. "It won't work."

The bell rang, and we both ducked into class. As

we slid into our seats, Ms. Carew wrote the quote of the day on the board.

There comes a point in life when you realize who really matters, who never did, and who always will, she wrote. I looked over at Sammie, who was busily putting her phone back where it belonged.

After school, Sammie and I walked home together. As we headed down the California Incline, the hill that leads from the Palisades down to the beach, she turned to me and said, "I might as well tell you now. We've decided to go to the game tonight. "

"We who?"

"Alicia, Sara, Etta, Bernard, and me. Will wanted to go, too, but his parents won't let him, so it'll be the five of us."

That was a surprise. Ever since she's been part of Truth Tellers, Sammie hasn't been interested in supporting school sports. Going to games isn't the kind of thing their group does.

"How come you decided that?" I asked her.

"We talked about it at lunch yesterday, and we all agreed that we really haven't given going to games a fair chance," she explained. "It's easy for us to say *that is so stupid* or *those kids are only into sports*. But then we'd be acting snotty and prejudiced like the SF2s, no offense."

I decided in the interest of making peace, I'd ignore her jab.

"Besides, Sara says she's drummed up the courage to break out one of her new looks tonight," she went on. "She's coming over before the game, and Alicia and I are going to put together her pirate look with GoGo's scarf and gold hoop earrings."

"Wow. She mentioned she was building up her courage, but it takes a whole lot of guts to take a chance like that at a football game."

"We told her to go for it."

"I'll look for her there," I said. "Maybe I can give her a little moral support."

"Careful," Sammie said. "You don't want to damage your precious reputation with the popular kids."

"Sammie," I said, trying to be really calm and patient "just because I choose to have different friends than you doesn't mean I'm a horrible person. I like Sara, and I'd like to be helpful to her. She's my friend, too."

As I said those words, I felt my stomach flip over on itself. How could I call myself a friend, when I had done the one thing she asked me not to do? That guilty feeling, the one I had been trying to squash all day came creeping back. It just wasn't going to go away.

The Game

....

Chapter 17

"I love Friday nights," my dad said as he picked up his car keys. "Nothing more fun than a high-school football game."

"You're not going, are you, Dad?" I asked, panic in my voice.

"Don't worry, Noodle. I'm going to keep him very busy right here," GoGo said. "He promised to help me skewer the kebabs for Bethany's party tomorrow night. Didn't you, Rick?"

"Let's see," my dad said. "Football game or kebab skewering. What should I do?"

"It's not even close, Dad," Ryan said. "Those kebabs need you."

My dad actually laughed. Everyone in our house was in a pretty good mood, even Sammie. She and

Alicia were busy getting Sara all fixed up.

Six of us—Sammie, Alicia, Sara, Ryan, his friend Winston Chin, and me—piled into my dad's minivan to drive to Pacific High School. When we got there, my dad tried to pull into the overflowing parking lot but he got stuck in a total traffic jam and couldn't go any farther.

We got out and went our separate ways. Sammie and her friends went to buy tickets in the general seating section. Ryan and Winston found some other guys from the volleyball team and went off with them.

I made sure my jacket was zipped up, and headed off to the snack stand. My friends were all there. We couldn't stop hugging and giggling. We were just so excited. Everyone gathered in a circle and Lauren counted to ten. At nine, we unzipped our jackets, and at ten, we took them off. Then we cheered.

A bunch of high-school kids, who were buying nachos and popcorn, turned to look at us.

"What do we have here?" a guy with bleached-blond hair asked.

"We're the Junior Waves." Lauren smiled proudly. She's awesomely pretty to begin with, but that smile kicked everything up a big notch.

"Sweeettt," he said. "You girls connected to Bethany's group?"

"Absolutely," Lauren beamed. You could tell that answer impressed him.

"Sweeettt," he repeated. "Welcome to Pacific High."

He walked away with his friends, who all turned around to give us a good-bye wave.

"How awesome was that?" Lauren squealed when they were far enough away not to hear us.

We all agreed that it couldn't have gone better. Just then, a girl wearing a Waves T-shirt ran by us. Lauren waved to her and called out, "Hi, Lizzy."

"What's up with those shirts?" she asked, looking us up and down, not in the nicest way.

"We're Junior Waves," Jillian answered. "We're hanging out with you guys at the game."

"Wow, I didn't know this was our night to babysit," Lizzy said. "Okay, follow me, kidlets."

We followed her into the stadium. She didn't get any nicer, but at least she didn't get any meaner.

"There they are!" Lauren said, pointing to a few rows of girls wearing The Waves signature turquoise-blue shirts with pink lettering. "I see Bethany."

"Wow," Brooke said. "Check out their seats."

The Waves were sitting right at the fifty-yard line, about ten rows back. The best seats in the stadium. The best place not only to watch the game, but to also see and be seen. There was a half-empty row behind them.

"Omigosh," Brooke said. "Are those for us? They saved us incredible seats."

"Of course they did," Lauren said. "Bethany's

taken care of everything." Then under her breath, she whispered to me, "What'd I tell you?"

We climbed up the bleachers and took our seats behind The Waves. Their club had about twenty girls, each one prettier than the next. Everyone except for Lizzy was nice, too.

"Hey, Juniors," some of the girls called to us. "Over here. Have a seat. Join the party!"

They were all snapping pictures of each other with their phones. When we reached our row, Bethany got out her phone and took a picture of all five of us with our arms around each other. She showed it to us, and we looked great, if I do say so myself.

"I'm going to post this on Instagram," she said. "What should I say?"

"Junior Waves rock," Lauren said.

"You got it," Bethany answered with a nod, and posted the picture without a moment's hesitation.

"Now we're famous," Jillian said. "Like TV stars."

"Pretty close," Bethany told her. "I've got a ton of followers. Everyone's going to see your picture, that's for sure."

Just then, Spencer Ballard, Ben Feldman, and the General, entered the stadium. My heart skipped a beat.

"We're over here," Brooke shouted at the top of her lungs. The boys looked up and waved, then headed up the steps to our row.

"Brooks, you can't shout like that," Lauren said. "We have to act like high-schoolers."

"Don't they shout, Lauren?"

"During the game, yes. They cheer. But not before the game."

What did Lauren do, read a book on high school etiquette? But as I looked around the stadium, I saw that she was right. Everyone was talking to their friends, sipping drinks, or checking their phones. I wondered if a lot of them were looking at the picture of us on Instagram that very moment. The thought made me giggle.

The guys filed into our row and took their seats. Spencer had to talk Ben Feldman into trading seats with him so he could sit next to me, but he did it.

"How's my favorite Junior Wave?" he said as he wedged in next to me.

If I had one word to describe how I was feeling at that very moment, it would have been "sweeettt!" Everything felt good, nothing annoyed me, not even Bethany who was busy being the queen bee, waving at all the guys who walked past and standing up a lot to make sure everyone could see how beautiful she was.

Her friend Lizzy seemed to be doing the same thing—standing, pointing, waving, hollering, doing everything she could to attract attention. She was right in front of me, so I could hardly miss it when suddenly she screamed, "Who or *what* is that?" She burst out laughing. "I think it's Captain Hook, I'm not kidding. She looks like a pirate."

I looked down to see Sammie and her friends

making their way up to the bleachers. Of course, the person Lizzy was referring to was Sara.

"Why do you think she's got that thing on her head?" Lizzy went on.

"Who can say why middle-schoolers do the things they do," the girl next to her said. "Maybe someone dared her to do it."

"It'd have to be a double dare for me to go out of the house looking like that," Lizzy said. "Or double double dare times a hundred. It's totally ridiculous."

I felt the blood rush to my face. I was furious. Why couldn't she just leave Sara alone? What should it matter to her if Sara looked like Captain Hook or Captain Crunch? It was none of her business.

"I think that girl looks very unique," I said to Lizzy. All she did was laugh and sing, "*Yo-ho, yo-ho, a pirate's life for me.*"

"Cut it out!" I snapped. "She happens to be an extremely nice and interesting person."

Lauren put her arm on mine. "Calm down," she whispered. "What are you so worked up about? You'll ruin the whole night. They're just goofing around. Let it be."

Spencer could see how agitated I was.

"I like Sara, too," he said. "They shouldn't talk about her like that."

"Don't worry about it, you two," Lauren said. "It's almost kickoff."

I was worried. Worried of course for Sara and that

people were going to say mean things to her face. That would hurt her so much. The thing about words is that once they're out there, you can't take them back. Mean words stay with you forever.

"Hey, Charlie," I heard Alicia call. I looked over and Sammie and her friends were standing in the aisle right near us. "Nice seats."

"Hi, Charlie," Sara said. She was smiling, and seemed really happy with herself. It killed me to know what Lizzy was saying behind her back. I shot her a thumbs-up and she gave me one back.

"Oh, I am so taking a picture of this," Lizzy said, snapping a picture of Sara with her cell phone.

"Why do you need a picture of her?" I asked.

"Just for fun," she said. "You have to admit, that's not an outfit you see every day."

"Well I think you should delete it," I said.

"Okay, okay," she said. "It's a stupid picture, anyway."

She did something with her phone, and then turned off the screen and put it away.

"Nice work," Spencer said to me. Then he smiled and took my hand.

Sammie and her friends found seats way up at the top of the bleachers just as the band came out and played the National Anthem. After that, the band launched right into the Pacific High fight song. Lauren was the only one of us who knew the words, but I managed to fake it pretty well. When the game started, The Waves taught us their two special cheers. The first time they stood up and did them on their own, but the second time, Bethany said we could do the cheers with them. I could feel everyone looking at us. Even the cheerleaders stopped their own cheers and tossed their pom-poms in the air when we were done.

When we sat down after the cheer, someone in back of me tapped me on the shoulder. It was the blond surfer guy.

"You guys really do rock," he said, holding up his phone to show me our picture on Instagram.

Underneath our caption, a bunch of people had written comments.

"Could I borrow your phone for a sec?" I asked.

He handed it to me, and I showed Lauren the comments. One said, "Cute mini waves," and another said, "Love that tween spirit." The one from a boy named Kahuna said, "Stoked to see these babes #juniorwaves" and the last one said, "My cousin's group, how cool are they?" That one was from Bethany, but the others were from random people who didn't even know us. We passed his phone quickly to the other girls, and each one in turn laughed out loud.

"Thanks," I said when I handed the phone back to the guy.

During the first half of the game, I found out that I was really interested in football. We're a tennis family, and Ryan watches a lot of basketball, so football was a whole new world to me. Spencer explained all the rules and strategies that I didn't know.

"You're a jock at heart, Diamond," he said. "Not many girls would be this curious."

At halftime, the score was tied at fourteen. Spencer left to go get some nachos, and Bethany told us to get up and come with her.

"Bathroom break," she said.

"I'm okay," I said. "I don't have to go."

"Honestly, Charlie," she sighed. "This isn't about peeing. This is about refreshing our hair and makeup. And trust me, little one, you could use it."

We all followed her and the other Waves to the girl's bathroom. Inside, it was jam-packed and the noise level was out of control. You had to shove your way in to get to the stalls, and getting to the mirror was almost impossible with girls lined up shoulder to shoulder applying lip gloss and touching up their mascara and stuff. I got separated from the other Junior Waves right away. For the first time that night, I felt like a middle-school kid shoved in between all these chattering high-school girls. I just kind of hunkered down in the crowd and tried to be inconspicuous.

"Well, of course I posted it," I heard Lizzy's voice in the crowd. "It was just too funny to resist."

"You're not going to believe the one I have," Bethany said back. "It's even funnier."

"Did you post it already?" Lizzy asked.

"Did I ever! There's going to be a million

comments. I can't wait to see them."

Two girls in Pacific High letterman jackets shoved themselves away from the mirror, creating a space for other girls. I jammed myself in there, trying to get close enough to hear the rest of the conversation, but I was elbowed out by another two girls in Taft jackets.

"Excuse me," I said to them. "It's really important that I get in here."

"Tough luck," one of them said. "We've been waiting for five minutes."

"Oh and by the way," the other one said, "your team is going down tonight!"

I struggled to get close, but by the time I got to the mirror, Bethany and Lizzy were halfway across the bathroom, on their way out. I elbowed my way through the crowded bathroom and finally reached the outside. They were surrounded by a bunch of cute high-school guys. They might have even been seniors—two of them had beards!

"Bethany, can I talk to you a minute?" I asked, tapping her on the shoulder.

"Use your head, little one," she said, laughing with the others. "Does it look like it's a good time for me to talk?"

Everyone laughed.

"This is really important," I said, yanking on her arm.

"No, Charlie," she said. She wasn't laughing now, she seemed mad. "What's going on here is important, not you. Come on, guys. The game's starting."

She hooked her arm through the arm of one of the bearded guys and walked away.

I didn't even wait for the other Junior Waves. I raced back to my seat. Spencer must have still been in the nachos line, and none of the other girls were back yet. But the person I wanted was there—the surfer dude sitting in back of me.

"Could I borrow your phone again?" I asked.

"No problem," he said, "Got to call your mom and dad to pick you up? Yeah, I remember those days. It gets better."

"No, I need to see your Instagram again," I said. "Can you show me how to go there?"

He punched in a few commands, and handed me his phone. The picture of us came up on the screen. There were a lot more comments, but I wasn't interested in that.

"Do you follow Lizzy whatshername?" I asked him.

He took the phone from me and went to Lizzy's account. There it was, front and center, the picture she had snapped of Sara in her scarf and earrings. Under it was the caption, "Can u believe it? Captain Hook showed up at our game tonight!!!"

I felt sick to my stomach. No one had posted any comments yet, but I knew they probably would.

"How about Bethany Wadsworth?" I asked him. "Do you follow her?"

"Who doesn't?"

He took the phone from me and went to her page. When I looked at the picture that came up on the screen, I couldn't believe my eyes. I thought I was actually going to throw up.

It was a shot of Sara, but not from the game. It was one of the "before" shots that Sammie and Alicia had taken of her. Her hair was pulled up on top of her head. She wasn't smiling. And of course, her ears were in plain view, sticking out almost to the edge of the picture. It was the most unflattering image of her you could ever imagine. And humiliating. Underneath was the caption Bethany had written. It said: "One word, folks. Dumbo."

I dropped the guy's phone and held my hands to my face.

"Hey, are you okay?" he said. He sounded a million miles away.

My mind was racing with a thousand ideas at once. Where could Bethany have gotten that picture? It was only on Sammie's phone. And no one had access to Sammie's phone, not even me. She kept it tucked away in the right zipper pocket of her purse.

Then it hit me. When we were at Etta's concert that afternoon, Sammie had specifically noticed that her phone was in the left pocket, out of its usual place. She chalked it up to just being forgetful, but there was another explanation, one that flooded into my head like a terrible, crashing wave.

I closed my eyes and remembered Lauren telling me how Bethany had given her one last initiation assignment to complete. Then I remembered her standing in the hall that afternoon, holding both our bags. She had been out there the whole time Sammie and I were helping Ms. Carew straighten up the room. Long enough to find Sammie's phone, go to her photo roll and send the picture of Sara to herself. Or to Bethany. Just as she had been asked to do. And then put the phone back in the wrong pocket!

But how did she know where to find Sammie's phone?

Then another image came to my mind, almost jolting me out of my seat. We were in my room, just before the ceremony, looking for my phone so we could play "We Are the Champions." I told Lauren to get it from my purse, and she knew just where to go. I heard her words in my head . . . "I know everything about you. You and Sammie both keep your phones in the left zipper pocket so Ryan can't get to them." And I remembered thinking . . . *No, Sammie keeps hers in the right pocket.*

How would Lauren and Bethany have known that the "before" pictures of Sara were there on Sammie's phone? How could they know that those pictures, showing in extreme close-up the very thing Sara was most ashamed of in the world, were so easy to get to?

And of course, there was only one answer to that.

It was me. Me, who told the group about the

pictures. Me, who betrayed the trust of not only Sara, but of Alicia and my sister. Me, and my big mouth. Me, and my need to belong.

It was me at the bottom of this whole nightmare.

I grabbed my jacket and made my way blindly to the aisle. As I was running down the steps, I ran smack into Spencer.

"Charlie, where are you going?"

"I'm sick," I lied. "I think I'm going to throw up. I have to go home."

I pushed him aside and tore out of the stadium, pushing my way through the throng of kids like I was fighting for my life. When I got outside the gate, I stood there in the parking lot and burst into tears, crying harder and longer than I ever had in my life.

Friendless

....

Chapter 18

"Maybe she won't find out," I said to GoGo, tears still streaming down my face. "Not many kids our age have Instagram, so maybe she'll never see it."

I had called GoGo to come get me from the game. She was the only person I could turn to in a time like this. In the car on the way home, I told her the whole story— how we formed the Junior Waves and had an initiation ceremony and how I had told Sara's secret even though I knew it was wrong.

We finally made it home and were alone in the clubhouse. Everyone was still at the football game except my dad, who had decided last minute to have coffee with a bunch of his old tennis pals until it was time to pick us up from the game.

"You have to confess everything," GoGo said,

putting a cup of hot chocolate down in front of me on the kitchen counter. "People make mistakes, Charlie. This was a big one. But you have to be brave and own up to your mistakes."

"So what do I tell Sara?" I asked. "That I'm sorry I ruined her life?"

"Speak from the heart, Noodle. That's all you can do."

"And what about Sammie? How do I explain this to her?"

"Same thing. Don't shift the blame to anyone else. Be brave and acknowledge what you did."

GoGo handed me a box of Kleenex. I sipped the hot chocolate and blew my nose constantly, staring at the clock and dreading the moment when they all walked in.

I heard a car pull up in the driveway, and my heart almost fell out of my chest.

"I can't do this, GoGo," I wailed.

"You can do anything you set your mind to," she said, giving me a tight hug.

I blew my nose one last time, and then stood up when I heard the door to the clubhouse slam shut. To my relief, it wasn't Sammie and the girls. It was Ryan.

"What are you doing here?" I asked. "I thought you were sleeping over at Winston's."

"I told his dad to just drop me off here," he said. "I thought Sammie and her friends could use a little support."

"Why?" I asked, so afraid to hear the answer.

"You didn't see the photos on Instagram? I thought by now everyone had seen them."

"You're on that Instagram thing, too?" GoGo asked.

"GoGo, I'm not a little kid anymore," he said. "I'm fourteen."

Ryan took out his phone and handed it to me. I looked at the Instagram picture of Sara, the one that Bethany had posted with the "Dumbo" caption underneath. Below it were a string of comments. A few of them were making fun of Sara. One said, "All the better to hear you with!" and another said, "She looks like a car with the doors open." But there were a lot of them that were kind of supportive. One of those said, "My brother has the same type of ears and he's cute." Another one said, "So what, we all have something we're embarrassed of." To my total shock, there were even a few that were critical of Bethany. One said, "Leave the girl alone, Beth" and another said, "Not ur buniness."

I handed the phone back to Ryan. "Not as bad as I thought it would be," I said.

"Most people are kind underneath," GoGo said. "They're not actively looking for opportunities to hurt people. But of course, that's not the point, is it, Noodle?"

I shook my head.

No, the point was that no matter how this turned

out, I was at fault. None of this would have happened if I hadn't opened my big mouth.

Ryan seemed confused. "What's Charles got to do with this?" he asked.

I couldn't stand it anymore. I didn't want to tell one more lie. And so I told him what I had done. Everything.

"Whoa," he said after I'd poured out my story. "This could get ugly. Maybe I should have slept over at Winston's after all."

"Actually, Ryan, that's not a bad idea," GoGo said. "I think Sammie and Charlie need to work through this by themselves."

"No problem," Ryan said. "I'm calling Winston now. See you guys in the morning. Oh, and good luck with this, Charles. Seriously."

He reached out and actually gave me a hug, a nice one. I felt better, but it was only temporary.

Too soon, I heard my dad's car pull into the driveway. I knew it was his because the brakes on his minivan squeak when he stops. I heard the doors slam . . . one, two, and three, the slider . . . then footsteps. There wasn't another human sound, not a peep. It was ghostly quiet out there. I stood up from the counter.

"Are you coming?" I asked GoGo.

"I'll be there if you need me," she said, taking my hand. "But you'll do what's right, Charlie. I trust you."

I took a deep breath. I thought I might actually faint, but with GoGo's help, I steadied myself and walked into the living room. I had no choice.

The first face I saw was Sara's, tear-streaked and pale. Her scarf was off and her poufy hair was sticking out wildly all around her head. Next to her was Sammie. Her eyes were red-rimmed from crying, too. Only Alicia wasn't in tears, but her face, usually so smiley and cheerful, was set in a fixed frown. My dad was the last to come in. You could practically see the gray smoke coming out of his ears. Without a word, he threw his keys on the coffee table and sat down. Everyone was staring at me.

"So I suppose you guys have all seen the picture?" I started, my voice shaking.

"Oh yeah, Charlie. We saw it," Sammie said. "We saw it on practically every single phone at the game. The guy next to us, the girl behind us, the couple in front of us. Apparently, Bethany has a lot of followers, which makes total sense because she's such a nice person."

I started to cry.

"I am so sorry for what happened to you, Sara," I said. "I never meant to hurt you."

"But this does hurt, Charlie," Sara said. "It hurts a

lot. On the way out of the stadium, I felt like everyone was staring at me. I felt like a freak."

The phrase "bearded lady in the circus" echoed in my head. It felt awful at the time and even worse now.

My dad sighed loudly and angrily.

"We're all sorry you feel that way, Sara," he said. "Deeply sorry. Everyone in this family is."

"So what exactly happened?" Sammie asked me. "Did you just go in my purse and send the photo to Bethany?"

"I never sent the picture to Bethany, I swear," I told her.

"Oh, so it just decided to send itself to Bethany's Instagram account? Right. That happens a lot, Charlie."

It was time for the truth, the whole truth. It didn't matter whether I was ratting out a friend or betraying a confidence. The lies had to stop. Enough was enough.

"Lauren sent it to Bethany," I said. "Then Bethany decided to post it."

"Oh and how did Lauren get it?" Sammie asked. "Let me guess. You gave it to her. Am I right?"

"No, you're not. She took it off your phone, during Etta's concert. That's why your phone was in the wrong zipper pocket."

"Well then tell me this, Sherlock Holmes." Sammie had crossed the room and was standing about two inches from my face. "If that's true, how did Lauren even know there was such a picture on my phone? Explain that if you can."

There it was—confession time. It was down to telling them my piece of the puzzle. I felt my throat close up and my mouth go dry.

I took a deep breath and started to talk. Before I knew it, everything was pouring out, words and tears all mixed together. I told them about the Junior Waves and the initiation ceremony on the beach, about how we each shared secrets, and about how they forced me to tell Sara's secret.

"They forced you?" Sammie said. "They didn't force you. You did it. You could have said no. You could have walked away and told them you didn't want to be in their stupid club, anyway. But you didn't, Charlie. You made a choice and it sucks."

I didn't try to explain it away or defend myself. She was right. I had made a choice, and it was the wrong one. So I did the only possible thing I had left to do.

"I'm so sorry, Sara," I said. "Deeply, truly, from the bottom of my heart sorry."

We all stood there in silence for what seemed like an eternity. At last, Sara stepped forward and walked over to me.

"I believe you," she said.

"I wish I could take it all back. I'd do anything to take it back."

Now Alicia was next to me.

"I feel how much you regret what you did," she said. "And I feel sorry for you, too. Sara isn't the only one here who's hurting."

"I really like you guys," I said, wiping my nose and tears on my jacket sleeve. "I don't know why I haven't been nicer to you."

"I know why," Sammie said. "Because you wanted to be one of those girls. You have ever since the day we moved here. You look up to them and think they're so hot because they're popular and rich and perfect. Well, what do you think of them now?"

"Lily wasn't part of this," I said. "And Brooke and Jillian just do anything Lauren says."

"That's obvious," Sammie said. "And guess what? So did you."

My dad stood up and went to the phone.

"You're not calling the police, are you Dad?" I asked.

"No, Charlie, of course not. You didn't do anything illegal, just disappointing. But there have to be consequences for this. Kids can't go around posting pictures with hateful comments. It's not right. I'm calling Lauren and Bethany's parents, to tell them what their daughters did."

"No, Dad! You can't do that!"

"Just watch me, Charlie."

"But Dad, can't we just think about this for a while? You always say you shouldn't do anything rash when you're angry. Besides, tomorrow is Bethany's party. If you tell her parents, it's going to ruin everything!"

"She should have thought of that before she did this," he said.

We listened as my dad made two phone calls. No one was home at Lauren's house, but Bethany's dad was there. When my dad explained to him that there was a big issue they had to discuss, Mr. Wadsworth said he would come over the next day and talk it through. He had to bring some party supplies over, anyway. My dad emphasized that this was a really important conversation. Mr. Wadsworth finally agreed to get in touch with Lauren's father and they'd all meet at the club at ten o'clock. My dad suggested they bring Bethany and Lauren, to get to the bottom of this.

So now I was going to have to face Lauren again. Already Sammie and her friends hated me. And tomorrow Lauren and the SF2 girls would officially hate me, too.

Truth and Consequences

....

Chapter 19

"Well, if it isn't the biggest rat ever," Lauren said as she walked onto the deck of the clubhouse the next morning. "Seems like we've done this same scene before, haven't we, Little Miss Tattletale?"

From her opening line, it was pretty clear how the rest of the meeting was going to go. It was exactly ten o'clock and we were all sitting at the table on the deck—my dad, Sammie, Sara, Sara's mom, and me.

I had hardly slept all night. The one time I did fall asleep, I had a dream about a clown wearing a scarf and hoop earrings. Then for no reason, he turned into a pirate who kept chasing me. Then he morphed into a pelican with a fish in his mouth, only the fish was me. I was happy when the sun rose in the morning and I could get up from the couch and start the day.

Anything had to be better than that dream.

Lauren slid onto the bench at the opposite end of the table. Her dad, Chip, who is a pal of my dad's (and the one who got him the job at the Sport Forty) came in from the parking lot carrying a newspaper under his arm. He sat down next to my dad.

"Stock market took a hit yesterday," he said. "Oh, and Lauren's mother can't make it this morning. She sends her apologies, but she and Carol Ann are getting their hair done for Bethany's party tonight. Hope it's okay if it's just me."

"It's fine, Daddy," Lauren said. "This shouldn't take long, anyway." She shot me a cold glance, and then looked away. "I don't suppose Ryan's here," she added.

"As it happens, he isn't," my dad said. "This isn't a social visit, anyway."

"Sounds like you're making a pretty big deal of this, Rick," Lauren's dad said. "Get a little perspective here. It's just kids who got themselves in a little jam."

Bethany's dad, Dennis Wadsworth, was the next to arrive, hurrying in and carrying a stack of plastic serving bowls in his arms.

"Let me just run into the kitchen and put these down," he said. "I remember the days when a birthday party was a simple affair."

Bethany took her seat at the far end of the table next to Lauren. She was holding her phone in her hand, which took a lot of nerve, given the topic of conversation this morning.

"Isn't anyone going to wish me a happy birthday?" she asked.

"I am," Lauren said. "Happy birthday, Beth."

When her father returned and we were all gathered around the table, my dad began.

"As I said last night on the phone, we have a problem that I think requires our attention," he said.

"Bethany has told me something about it," her dad said. Then looking at Sara, he said, "And I'm terribly sorry if you got your feelings hurt in any way, young lady."

I noticed Sara's mom reach out and squeeze Sara's hand.

"Like I always say to Lauren," her dad, Chip, said, "we all have to watch what we say and do with these phones."

He seemed to think that was the end of the conversation, but my dad wasn't letting it go.

"Did your daughters tell you exactly what happened?" he asked. "That Lauren pressured Charlie into telling a secret that wasn't hers to tell, holding her membership in the Junior Waves over her head?"

Chip looked surprised. I saw him shoot a questioning glance to Lauren, who just shrugged and said, "He's making it sound like a bigger deal than it was."

"And that Lauren took Sammie's phone without permission and stole the picture and sent it to

Bethany," my dad went on. Then turning to Dennis, he added, "And your daughter posted it on a photo-sharing site with a cruel comment."

"Can I see this posting?" Dennis asked.

Bethany handed him her phone, and I saw him flip to the screen.

"We thought it was funny, Daddy," Bethany said. "Some people just can't take a joke. I didn't know she was so sensitive. I'm sure I'm not the first one to call her Dumbo."

Sara winced like someone had punched her.

"Do not say those words ever again, young lady," Sara's mom said, her dark eyes full of anger. "Apologize right now."

"Okay, okay," Bethany said. "Don't get all in a twist about it. So sorry."

Obviously, she couldn't have cared less about her apology.

Dennis passed the phone to his brother Chip, who looked at the picture and scrolled through all the comments. I looked over at Sara to see how she was taking this. Her eyes were looking down at the planks on the redwood table, studying them intently. She never looked up.

"Can we go now, Uncle Chip?" Bethany said, taking back her phone. "We still have a ton of stuff to do to get ready for the party."

She stood up and turned to the gate, but her father took her arm and stopped her.

"Sit down, young lady," he said. "I'm going to tell you a story—perhaps one that I should have told you before. Pay attention."

Bethany reluctantly flopped down on the bench and put on her most bored look ever.

"When Chip and I were growing up, there was a kid who lived down the block," her father began. "He was a short kid, and I'm ashamed to say, we made terrible fun of him. Developed all sorts of names for him. Peanut. Shrimp. Shortypants. Some a lot meaner than that."

"Just put up a flag when this is going to get interesting," Bethany said.

"Well, when we got to high school, lo and behold, this short kid sprouted up. In fact, he sprouted up quite a bit, so much so that he made the basketball team at UCLA."

"Which we did not," Chip added. "Remember, Rick, we barely made the junior varsity team in high school."

His brother held up his hand for Chip to be quiet, then continued his story.

"So this short kid played pro basketball," Dennis said. "Made some good money, invested well. Do you know who he is now?"

"Kobe Bryant?" Lauren guessed.

"No. Even better. He's the owner of an NBA team. And my boss."

Bethany looked shocked.

"That's right, Bethany. I work in the main office, and I have a fine position. But my boss is that kid I used to call Peanut. He proved to be a bigger man than me in a lot of ways, not the least of which was hiring me when he bought the team."

Sara looked up from the table and smiled. Bethany's dad looked at her and smiled back.

"So you see, neither you nor Lauren has the right to make fun of anyone," he said, "especially not this lovely young lady sitting across from us. I'm disappointed in both of you."

Lauren's Dad seemed more concerned with practical matters.

"Do you think the school officials already know about this?" he asked. "I'd hate for our girls to have any repercussions at school."

"If they don't already know, I assure you they will," Mrs. Berlin said, "because I plan to tell them myself. Kids can't go around cyberbullying other kids. It's unacceptable. Do you have any idea how embarrassing this was to my daughter? How much something like this hurts?"

Mrs. Berlin put her arm around Sara. The moment her mother touched her, Sara burst into tears. Not just the flowing kind, but the sobbing kind, the way I had cried last night.

Bethany's dad looked like he was going to cry, too.

"This is what you've done," he said to Bethany, shaking his finger in the air. "And you too, Lauren.

Take a good look and then tell me how you feel about yourselves."

"We didn't do anything *that* bad," Bethany said. "We were just having fun."

Mr. Wadsworth was on his feet now. He was tall, and he towered over Bethany.

"You had fun at someone else's expense," he said. "In my book, that is not fun, that's cruelty. Do you hear me, Bethany? Are you listening, Lauren?"

"You don't have to shout, Daddy. We're not deaf."

"I participated, too," I said softly. "I was the one who started the whole thing."

Mr. Wadsworth wheeled around and looked at me for the first time.

"And how do you feel about what you've done?" he asked.

"Terrible. I was wrong, so totally wrong. I wish I could take back everything I did, but I can't. So I'm just going to have to try to be better."

"Well, you're a brave girl," Bethany's dad said to me. "Half the battle of doing the right thing is owning up to it when you've done the wrong thing. I wish I felt certain that Bethany and Lauren understood that."

"Okay, Daddy," Bethany whined. "I get it. Now can we stop talking about this?"

"Yes, we can. But I hope you understand, Bethany, that there are going to be consequences. At home and at school."

"What do you mean by that?" Bethany said, rising to her feet.

Suddenly, Mrs. Berlin stood up to face her. She looked her square in the eyes, in a way that made even Bethany uncomfortable. When she spoke, her voice was angry but controlled.

"You could be expelled, young lady," she said. "Many schools demand that a student who posts an inappropriate picture with hateful messages must leave."

"Like for good?" Bethany said.

"That's usually what expelled means," Sammie said.

"What about me?" Lauren asked. "They're not going to kick me out, are they?"

For the first time ever, she sounded shaky and insecure.

"I can't imagine your principal will look kindly on your behavior," my dad said.

"Wait . . . does that mean I can't be a Junior Wave?" she cried. Now she seemed really upset.

"I think you'd better wave good-bye to The Waves," Sammie said. "Junior, senior, or any other kind."

"You don't know that," Lauren said with a scowl.

"Yeah," Bethany added. "You don't know anything, you creep."

Mrs. Berlin gathered her sweater in one hand and took Sara by the other.

"This whole experience has been very hurtful to

my child," she said. "I just hope you people will do something so no one else has to suffer like Sara has. Now if you'll excuse us. We've had enough of this."

Mrs. Berlin guided Sara across the deck.

"Stand up tall," I heard her say to Sara. "You have nothing to be ashamed of."

"I'll come over to your house as soon as we're done here," Sammie said, running over to give Sara a hug.

I practically tripped over myself to get to her before she reached the gate.

"Sara," I said, taking both her hands in mine. "I hope you'll forgive me. I'm going to work really hard to deserve your friendship."

"I'll try, Charlie."

When Sammie and I came back to the table, Bethany's dad was pacing up and down the deck, holding his cell phone to his ear.

"Well, can you please tell her it's urgent that we speak," he barked into the phone. "I don't care if she's in the middle of a blow dry."

"What are you doing, Daddy?" Bethany asked.

He didn't answer, just spoke into the phone.

"Hello, Carol Ann," he said. "The party's off. I'm canceling it."

"No, Daddy! You can't do that!" Bethany shouted, jumping up and stomping her foot. "We have hats and party favors and everything."

"I can and I have," he said to her. "If I were you, I'd spend more time figuring out where you're going to complete high school than thinking about party favors."

"Wow, this is intense," Lauren said.

Her dad, Chip, stood up and headed for the gate. "First the stock market takes a hit, then this," he said. "What a week. Come on, Lauren. You're going to have to get re-acquainted with the inside of your room."

Suddenly, Lauren whirled around and shook her finger at me.

"This is all your stupid fault!" she yelled. "I wish we had never invited your into our club in the first place. We never really wanted you, anyway. We just used you so we could get the charter. I should have known you'd rat us out again. You are so out of our group. Forever."

I couldn't even begin to get a word out to answer her back. But Sammie could.

"Is this the best you can do, Lauren?" she yelled. "Blame other people for what you've done. Well I have an idea. Why don't you stop blaming everyone else and take a hard look at yourself for a change?"

"I do look at myself," Lauren shouted back. "And I look great. A whole lot better than you two losers."

Lauren got up to leave, but Sammie followed her to the gate. She was on fire!

"My sister is way too good for you!" she said. "You will never be half the person she is. So just go home and enjoy your stay in your room. I'd say see you around school, but it sounds like you may be leaving

Beachside prematurely."

Lauren turned and stomped out of the club, her father following behind her.

"The girl's got her mother's temper," was all he said as he left.

Sammie came back to the table and flopped down in a chair. She was practically shaking all over.

"Thanks for saying that, Sams. I didn't deserve it."

"Yes, you do. You messed up big-time. But I know your heart's in the right place. Sara knows that, too."

"And I'm going to prove it to her."

"How?" she asked.

"Just wait and see."

The Real Hats Off!

....

Chapter 20

"GoGo," I said. "Do you still have all the kebabs?"

"Of course. They've been marinating since last night. I'm afraid we're going to be eating kebabs until they come out of our ears."

"And the mini quiches, too?"

"I'll have to freeze them, I guess. They won't be as good, but at least I won't waste my good cooking on that awful girl and her friends."

"If it's okay with you, GoGo," I said, "I have another plan for that food. Wait right here."

I ran to my room and called Spencer. I felt I owed him an explanation for bolting last night. But I didn't have to explain anything because he knew all about what had happened. Apparently, everyone did. News like that spreads fast.

"What are you doing now?" I asked him.

"Waiting to see what you're doing," he answered in a typical Spencer way.

"Can you come over? I have a project I need help on."

"Sure, I'll come. But you should call Lily, too. She's been texting me all morning to see if you're okay."

"You mean she still wants to talk to me?"

"Call her and find out," he said.

I was really nervous when I called Lily. I like her so much, and I really didn't want to lose her friendship.

"Oh, Charlie," she said, a whole big gush of words falling out of her mouth at once. "I'm so sorry about everything that happened. How are you? And how is Sara? Does she feel awful? What can we do to make it up to her?"

"Did you say *we*?" I asked her.

"Of course."

"You mean you're still going to talk to me, even after I ratted out Lauren?"

"I'm done with Lauren," she said.

"Jillian and Brooke, too?"

"That's up to them," Lily told me. "They always do what Lauren says, anyway, so if they want to stay with her, fine. But I see a lot of great things for you and me in the future."

"Can the future start right now?" I asked her. "As in . . . can you come over at three thirty today? Oh, and can you bring all the hats for Bethany's party?"

"I hear the party's off."

"It is. I mean it was. I mean it is. You'll see. Just come over and bring the hats, okay?"

"I'll be there."

Next I went to Sammie, who was getting ready to go over to Sara's house.

"You have to do something really important for me," I told her. "Can you get Sara back here at four o'clock?"

"Why?"

"Because I have to start being her friend," I said. "And four o'clock seems like a good time to do that."

"You're really not going to tell me what this is about?"

"You'll know at four o'clock," I told her. "Oh, and tell Sara to wear the pirate scarf and earrings. I think it looked great on her."

When Spencer arrived, he and I put together a big list of telephone numbers and divided up making the calls. I called Alicia and her parents, Will Lee and Etta, Ryan who was still at Winston Chin's. Spencer called Ben Feldman and Bernard and these kids named Devon and Keisha who are in Truth Tellers, too.

If you're wondering why we were making these calls, then you haven't really been paying close attention. Put the clues together, my friend. The party food, the party hats, a guest list that included all of Sara's friends. That's right, you guessed it. I was transforming Bethany's party into a big celebration

for Sara. After what she had been through, the girl
deserved a parade in her honor.

Spencer and GoGo and I cooked all afternoon.
Esperanza and Candido insisted on coming over to
help us. We had kebabs and quiche coming out of
our ears! My dad said he was proud of me and lighted
tiki torches on the beach. Sean and Jared were there
working, and he asked them to sweep the deck and set
up all the chairs and tables. I don't think I need to tell
you that they had plenty of attitude about that!

At one point in the afternoon, Lauren dropped by
to visit them. Personally, I think they had told her that
there were big plans going on. She hung around and
tried to check things out, without ever talking to me.
But I didn't have any interest in talking to her, either,
so finally she stomped off, saying in a really loud voice
that she had better things to do.

You know what? I don't think she had anything to
do at all.

I had all the guests arrive at 3:30 p.m. Lily came
with a carload of hats and we laid them all out along
the table. They looked amazing. There were turbans
and hard hats, straw hats and baseball caps, Girl Scout

beanies and black velvet hats with lace, all decorated with Lily's unique touch. Of course, Ryan picked the hard hat with the pink velvet bows. So typical. And speaking of typical, little Will Lee picked the tallest cowboy hat you've ever seen. It must have added six inches to his height.

"I know you older women like tall men," he said, giving me an actual wink.

Honestly, Will. Get a hold of yourself.

I wore the red-jeweled turban, and Spencer looked pretty cute in a vintage Yankees baseball cap. As each guest came in, I told them to pick out a hat to wear. When almost everyone was there, my dad left to go pick up Sammie and Sara. By four o'clock, all the food was set out beautifully on the tables, the torches were lit, and the guests were all decked out in their fancy fabulous hats.

All that remained was to organize the group for Sara's arrival. I asked Spencer if he would help me get everyone's attention. He jumped up onto a chair, put two fingers in his mouth, and let out a shrill whistle.

"Listen up, you guys," he hollered. "Charlie's going to explain what's about to happen."

He pulled me up onto the chair with him.

"Okay, everyone," I said. "We're going to have to be very quiet until Sara gets here. I'll give you a signal when I hear the car pull up. Then I'll count to three and when Sara comes in, everyone throw your hats in the air and shout HATS OFF TO SARA!"

"Nicely done," Spencer said, jumping off the chair and helping me get down, too.

"You had a rough week, Charlie," he said.

Then he put his hand on my face and leaned in to kiss me. It wasn't a huge kiss, but it wasn't a little one, either. It was a perfect, medium-size kiss. I would have liked it to go on longer, but we were interrupted by the sound of a car pulling up in the parking lot.

"Okay, she's here," I whispered to the crowd. "Everybody ready?"

We waited in silence, and within a minute, the gate opened, and Sammie came in followed by Sara.

"One ... two ... three ... ," I yelled.

"HATS OFF TO SARA!" the whole group screamed at once. We tossed all our wild, crazy, colorful hats in the air and broke into huge applause. It was an amazing sight.

Sara put her hands up to her face and looked around. We were all cheering and shouting and throwing our hats.

You're not going to believe what she did. Reaching up to her head, she pulled off the scarf. Her hair was tucked on top of her head, and you could plainly see all of her—including her ears. But mostly what you saw was her smile, big and glowing.

As she stood there in front of us, I felt proud to be her friend. She was happy. She was beautiful. And we loved her just the way she was.

I watched everyone gather around Sara. I was

overcome with emotions of all kinds and I burst into tears—tears of happiness and tears of sadness. Sadness about what I had done, happiness about what I had learned.

As Sara circulated among all the kids there, Sammie found me and came over to talk.

"It was really nice of you to throw this party for Sara," Sammie told me

"I have a lot to make up for," I said. "I made some bad choices . . . about Sara and about you, Sams."

"Yeah, I believe you owe me a dinner," Sammie said.

"Tomorrow night," I smiled. "Sausage and mushroom pizza at Barone's. Just you and me."

"You better not cancel this time."

"No way," I said. "I learned my lesson. There's no one more important than you, Sammie."

A loud hoot went up from somewhere in the crowd. We looked over and saw that a little crowd had formed around Ryan, who was doing some of his signature power moves on the deck. He's got this robot thing that he thinks is really cool, although Sammie and I think he looks like a sick chicken when he does it. No one cared, though. In fact, dancing right there with him was Etta, who looked like an even bigger, sicker chicken than Ryan. Everyone was gathered around them, clapping and cheering and having a great time. Ryan threw his arms around Etta and gave her a giant robotic twirl.

"You're kidding me," Sammie said. "Ryan and Etta?"

"Why not?" I said. "She's pretty cool."

"Listen to you," Sammie said. "Suddenly you're a big fan of my so-called weird friends. I never thought that would happen."

"I've learned a lot in the last few days," I said. "And I'm sorry I misjudged your friends. They're great."

"So, Charlie, does that mean you're going to become a Truth Teller? Come to our meetings and events and stuff?"

I hesitated.

"Well, maybe not all the time," I answered.

"It's the humming, isn't it?" Sammie said.

"It doesn't help. And neither does having to deal with Will Lee and his sexy sixth-grade moves."

We both burst out laughing. Whoa, that felt good.

"So does this mean we're friends again?" I asked, when we were all laughed out.

"Oh, better than friends, Charlie. We're sisters. Forever and ever."

Automatically, we both reached up and did three taps on the chest, right over our hearts. It's our secret love sign. GoGo says we've been doing it since we were in the crib together.

We threw our arms around each other and hugged until I thought our arms were going to fall off.

"Hey, I want in on that," Lily said, coming over and throwing an arm around both of us.

"Me too," Alicia said, joining in.

"Wait a minute. That's my hug," Sara said.

"Oh no it's not, it's mine," Etta said.

And before you know it, a whole bunch of us were together in a giant group hug. Sammie's friends. My friends. All of us. It didn't matter if you had green hair or a good body or fancy clothes or the right makeup or danced like a sick chicken. There was no judgment, no one to impress.

We were all simply enjoying being together and being what we were, good friends.

I double dare you to find anything more wonderful than that.

Reread your favorite
moments with Charlie
and Sammie!

almost
identical

growing up and growing apart

by lin oliver

I love my sister. She's always there for me when I screw up. Of course, I'm there for her, too, but she doesn't screw up nearly as often as I do.

almost identical

Two-faced

growing up and growing apart

by lin oliver

"Hey, didn't you guys used to be identical?" Ryan said.
"Almost identical," we both said at once.

almost identical

double-crossed

growing up and growing apart

by lin oliver

Charlie and I always dress alike when we play tennis
because our dad thinks it's good strategy. "Makes your
opponent think she's seeing double," he says.